ABOUT THE AUTHOR

Claire Merchant is an Australian author and storyteller. She is best known for her collection of fantasy, contemporary, and romance novels set in fictional South Coast. In 2018, Claire was voted one of the '50 Great Writers You Should Be Reading' by The Authors Show.

MISTRY BY MOONLIGHT

...Such is Fate

ALSO BY CLAIRE MERCHANT

For anyone who didn't recognise the stranger in the mirror

Acknowledgements

Firstly, I'd like to extend a big thank you to my all friends and colleagues, particularly Lauren, Elysia, and Lina. Your support, encouragement, and inspiration mean more to me than I can put into words. Also, thank you to Louisa for giving me strength and showing me hope when I couldn't see it for myself.

Credit must also go to my Year 10 English teacher, Tanya Srzich; my university mentor, Dr Angeline O'Neill; and my Aunty Lisa for opening up the world of words to me. You all inspired me to engage in the magic of books at different stages of my life, and you all hold a special place in my heart.

To everyone who has challenged me, and all the artists, musicians and authors who inspire me: you made me the person I am and taught me to trust in myself and my imagination.

To everyone who reads this book: I hope you can take something away from it, even if it's just the belief that you are enough just as you are – in whatever form you choose. Don't let anyone tell you otherwise.

Last but definitely not least, thank you so much to my Mum, Dad, my brother Paul, and the rest of my amazingly awesome and spellbinding family who have always allowed me to be myself and live in my imaginary world – I love you, I adore you, to the Moon and back.

Be yourself. Be enough. Be kind.

Claire x

Preface
The Beginning of the End

I died when I was six. Drowned. I was out for a little over two minutes before my father, Doctor Mistry, managed to get me breathing again. But even that didn't compare to now. I hadn't seen death, really *seen* it until now. It was different from what I imagined, what I remembered. It wasn't peaceful or reminiscent of life; it was cold, empty, and devoid of happiness, and any other human feeling. It was lonely, and unromantic, and completely, downright terrifying. Somewhere at the back of my mind, I thought of the satire of how I would come to die now, after having gone through so much to be safe from the monsters that I never knew existed only hours before. Now, when things seemed possible, it would end almost as quickly as they'd started. But that's what happens when you're marked with death – it's inevitable, a ticking time bomb. *Tick, tick, tick,* breathe in, breathe out; which would be my last?

I ran with as much force I could muster, feeling the balls of my feet push off the ground with raw energy, the shot of survival adrenaline pushing me further and faster than I'd ever ran before until my lungs burnt fiercely from the exertion. My chest felt as though someone had poured kerosene over it, and dropped a match on my flesh, and the only thing keeping me from collapsing from the pain was the knowledge of what was behind me. I knew if I hesitated, even for a second, that the monster pursuing me would indisputably kill me. I was alone now, and it was up to me to keep myself alive. After all this time, remaining hidden from the world, I almost couldn't believe this is how it all would end. It all seemed unfair considering everything I'd been through in the past year to get here. It felt too ironic to me that if I hadn't worked so hard for my present life, I'd probably be dead already. I could never have run like this a year ago. But then, perhaps I wouldn't have been marked with death in the first place if I hadn't have left South Coast to make that life-altering change.

A blood-curdling scream sounded around me, and I tried not to let it distract me from my rhythmic paces. If I stopped now, it would all have been for nothing. Even if, realistically, I knew that I was not expected to survive this, and that realisation washed over me in a kind of morbid relief. It would soon be over.

Over.

Dead.

I felt my left leg buckle under the strain of exertion, and let out a pained whimper. No, I couldn't think that way, I owed it, in the very least, to *him* to keep running. If I gave up now, I'd never see his face again, or feel his hand stroke my cheek, or hear the way he said my name as if it was the most sacred word ever uttered. I threw myself forward, hearing the leaves and debris crackle behind me, and knew I was almost out of time.

The moisture began to overflow from my eyelids, as I heard the steps grow nearer behind me, my head pounding with my heavy heart.

This was it, I was going to die.

I tried to push harder, but it was no use. I could feel my resolve weakening. To think that, up until recently, my biggest problem was the fact I couldn't decide between the one I'd always wanted, the one who wanted me, and the one I could never have. To think that now, after I'd finally made the decision, and achieved the life for myself that I'd always wanted, that it should be my time to die. At least it was a noble death.

Well, I guess you can't live forever, no matter how hard you tried. This year was supposed to be my year – the year it all happened for me. But, instead, it ended up being my last. Who would have thought I'd see the light just when time was rapidly running out?

Such is fate.

Phase One
The Silver Dagger

I gazed out the small oval window of the aircraft at the Full Moon and took a deep breath. I exhaled slowly as my heart thumped unevenly in my chest, and I waited for the seatbelt sign to disappear so I could leave the plane. Home. South Coast. Finally after a near twenty-four-hour delay at my stopover.

I'd left for Europe in the summer holidays separating my third and fourth year of veterinary science at university, and ended up deferring study for a year to stay. At the time, my decision hadn't exactly thrilled my parents since my father, Doctor Jackson Mistry, had arranged an internship for me in Half Moon Bay, a small country town just north of South Coast City, for my first semester back. I didn't regret passing up the opportunity though, and while the internship may have been priceless for my career aspirations, Europe had been an invaluable learning curve for my personal growth. During my time away, I was able to live in a different world where no one knew me; where I wasn't Jesse's overweight twin sister, and where I could re-establish myself, and really figure out who I was. For a year, I lived in Italy, moving around every couple of months and spending the odd long weekend in France. I'd grown up a lot in that year after being forced into independent living, and I had changed more than just mentally and emotionally since I'd been gone. Before I'd left, I was invisible, miserable, depressed, and devoid of hope. The day I'd decided I needed to leave, I had hit rock bottom with brute force. I remembered the darkness of that plane trip to Paris. That day I'd cried every last tear that was left in me, and I'd made a promise to myself then and there that no one would ever make me feel like I wasn't good enough. I never wanted to feel like I didn't deserve happiness just because I didn't look like everyone else. For as long as I could remember, I had been ashamed of my appearance. I looked in the mirror and saw a stranger staring back at me, a girl trapped in a body that didn't belong to her. I remembered crying myself to sleep, and praying that I wouldn't wake the next morning, or maybe one day I'd discover I had a disorder which meant I was overweight for reasons beyond my control. Before that day, I had tried everything to lose weight and failed more times than I could count on one hand. That day, I began to formulate a plan to claw my way back up. The first thing I did was take control, which meant removing myself from the things that I'd used to hide behind. So, I decided a change was needed. I'd always wanted to travel, to experience Europe in its timeless culture and beautiful scenery, so I fled South Coast.

Every day I spent away, I'd made a conscious effort to meticulously plan every single piece of food that I put into my mouth, formulating the difference between grains, and milk products, between proteins, and fats. I measured, weighed, and rationed my food, ensuring that my calorie intake was adequate to function without making me store in starvation, and then exercised to the point of my physical exhaustion. Luckily, the most effective mode of transport in France and Italy was by foot or bicycle.

It took a lot of effort and hard work over those eleven months, but by the time I began my long flight home, I had shed enough fat to take me down four dress sizes. For the first time in my life, the girl I saw when I looked into the mirror was one I could identify with. It was a long time coming, and after twenty-two years on this planet, I was finally accepting of myself.

Of course, with my new body came a new found confidence, and when I met Leo, the scars from my childhood of being laughed at seemed to somehow heal in the way he looked at me. We forged an unforgettable bond in the less than twenty-four hours of knowing each other, and it was those final moments with him that I'd remember most vividly from my time abroad…

"I miss you already," he whispered in his thick Italian accent, the memory of him tucking a piece of my long brown hair behind my ear swirling in my busy mind. His voice echoed in my subconscious. *"Do not go; stay with me."*

I recall smiling shyly at the tempting offer. *"You know I can't, Leo, I have uni and my family and reality to get back to."*

"I wish we had more time. I wish I could have taken you out properly," he sighed, kissing my hand tenderly. *"Such is fate."*

I shook my head. *"It's better this way."*

"How can you say that? We have only had one day together. I still do not know you as well as I would like to," he replied, my answer clearly offending him. I'd felt a small sense of delight in the fact.

"You know more than most people," I'd answered honestly. People didn't normally take the time to know me unless it was to use me to get close to Jesse. *"What do you want to know?"*

"Well, um, what is your favourite colour?" he whispered, a note of pleading desperation in his tone. It was as if the realisation that this was ending before it had the chance to begin was hitting him full force.

"Green – verde," I said. *"Though it changes; this week it's green."*

"Verde, sì." He nodded and then sighed. *"You are so beautiful, Taylor…"*

I exhaled at the memory of my last night in Rome. It had been only then that my transformation felt complete; when I felt like maybe I *was* good enough after all. I hadn't seen any of my family or friends in the year I'd been away, and I knew that my makeover would come as a shock to them since twenty-two kilos was a substantial difference to anyone's physique. The thought of going back scared me more than I allowed myself to admit because I didn't know the new me in my old life. The world felt different now, and my former reality was an alternative one that I never wanted to visit again. My whole fundamental make-up had been completely made-over like I'd been irrevocably changed, mind, body, and soul – character shaped a little sharper from the experiences I'd faced, and

17

people I'd met while I was away. My entire world that had been lit fluorescently, now felt like it was fading back to black, like a New Moon replacing a full one, with the sky being none the wiser.

My awareness faded back into my current aeroplane setting as the seatbelt light blinked off, and my attention snapped back to reality – to what I now had to face. Jesse.

"Oh my… geez, Tay, look at you," my twin brother gushed, running his tanned hand through his ash blond hair. "You look amazing."

I smiled bashfully as I stepped forward to hug him with the arm not attached to my luggage. Jesse, on the other hand, wrapped both arms entirely around me, lifting me off my feet in a tight squeeze.

"Man, I've missed you," he whispered into my ear. "I'm so glad you're home."

He released me and pulled back to look at me again, shaking his head incredulously.

"I missed you too, Jess," I answered, unable to say that I was truly happy to be home. I had missed him more than anything or anyone though; regardless of us living in different social worlds growing up, Jesse and I were as close as twins get.

"You're quiet," Jesse said. "Is everything okay?"

"Yeah," I sighed. "I'm just tired. It was a long flight and I can't seem to sleep on planes."

Jesse nodded, and turned me towards the moonlit darkness outside, leading me towards his black Mercedes.

The lights on the freeway flashed sporadically overhead as Jesse drove us homeward, and I gazed absently into the passenger side mirror, watching as they passed as if each illuminating my homecoming.

"So, what's it like?" Jesse asked, stealing a glance over at me. "You must feel different, do people treat you different?"

"Yes, I suppose." I shrugged. "I don't know, I *look* different, but I thought I'd *feel* different, like, better or more comfortable in my skin, but it's just the same."

Jesse frowned. "You didn't think losing the weight would change you into someone else did you?"

I smiled weakly. "I kind of hoped it would. But all the insecurities are still there. I'm exactly the same just with less to look at. It's weird."

"That's a good thing," he said. "We don't want you to change; we love you the way you are – however you are."

"Yes, *you* do," I sighed, rolling my eyes. "But now I don't know whether people… guys… want to be with me for me, or because of how I look. At least before I knew who my friends were, though they were few, they were loyal. I don't know if I want to be around people who didn't see me when I felt completely invisible."

As the lights drifted overhead, my gaze caught sight of a sepia coloured animal limping by the side of the road. It was as if all my veterinary training came flooding back and I jumped up in my seat.

"Pull over, Jesse!" I gasped, clutching at the door handle.

"What? Taylor, are you serious—?"

"Pull over now," I repeated as he swerved the car. I told myself I wouldn't have leapt from the moving vehicle, but I wasn't entirely convinced of the fact, not that it mattered.

"Are you going to tell me…?" Jesse started, but I was already half out the car. "Tay!"

"He's hurt," I called back over my shoulder, gesturing towards the obviously wounded animal.

"Taylor, are you crazy? Do you have a death wish?" Jesse barked. "Come back to the car! Taylor!"

I waved Jesse away and continued towards it, as the large wolf turned its hypnotic eyes towards me, and my advance was momentarily suspended by the iced green of their colour. My pace slowed warily at the wild animal's stare, but then its legs buckled from under it, and I noticed the shining silver weapon projecting from its right shoulder blade. I hurried over, sinking beside it, and gently stroked the animal's fur as it whined in pain.

"Oh, God," I breathed, pulling off my jacket and wrapping my hand around the handle of the protruding silver dagger.

"I'm sorry, this might hurt a little," I whispered more for my own benefit. The animal blinked in my direction, and there was something that resembled comprehension in its eyes. I felt it intake a breath as I pulled the weapon free from its body. I then pressed the fabric over the gaping wound.

"It's deep," I mused aloud. I was glad that, of all people, I was here to help the animal. Though, I'd only completed three of my five years of veterinary science. "I might have to—"

My inane muttering was cut off by a blood-curdling screech, and I reflexively covered my ears from the high-pitched noise. I turned to see the glass of the car windows and lights shatter behind me, as a flash of white flittered passed my back.

"Taylor!" Jesse called again, though unlike me, he seemed unaffected by the noise.

I couldn't move and my head pulsed with pressure as the scream continued. I squeezed my eyes closed just in time to feel four nails sink into the skin of my left shoulder, and then they shot open as the wolf sprang to life, knocking me onto my back as it leapt at whatever was behind me and then disappeared into the adjacent shrubbery. The screaming suddenly ceased, and I blinked in shock before grabbing my jacket and the silver dagger, and running back to the car.

"What were you thinking? What was that?" Jesse asked angrily as I darted into the passenger seat, eager to get away from whatever was stalking me. The car was already pulling back onto the road as I closed the door, the pieces of glass flying from the bonnet as he drove. My bloodstained hands shook with fright for the remainder of the silent trip home.

When Jesse pulled up the driveway to our childhood home, the front door swung open almost instantly, and my mum and dad ran to meet us. Their pace slowed as they momentarily assessed the damage to Jesse's Mercedes.

"What happened?" my mother, Charlie, gasped. "Are you two all right?"

"Hi, Mum." I smiled weakly, twisting my bloodstained hands around each other. She looked up at me and smiled widely.

"Taylor, honey, look at you! My baby girl," she gushed walking forward to hug me. "You're tiny."

I exhaled. "I've been getting fit."

"I'll say," she sighed and looked back to my father. "Jack, doesn't she look incredible?"

"Beautiful, as always," my father answered as he stepped forward to hug me. "We missed you."

"I missed you too, Dad." I smiled weakly.

"Jesse, are you going to tell us what on earth happened to your car?" Mum asked. "And Taylor, why are your hands covered in blood?"

"It's not my blood," I replied instantly, and then bit my lip. "But it's my fault; sort of. I saw an injured wolf on the side of the highway and tried to help it."

"A wolf? Taylor, honestly!" she sighed.

"How do you explain the broken windows then?" Dad asked, his forehead creasing with thought.

"I think that had something to do with the screaming," I mused, glancing back to Jesse, who looked less than impressed about the damage to his car.

"What screaming?" Jesse asked. "I didn't hear any screaming."

"You didn't?" I frowned. "Are you being serious?"

Jesse shrugged impatiently.

"Well, how do *you* explain the windows breaking then?" I challenged.

"Beats me," he answered. "The whole thing was bizarre. I really don't know *what* you were thinking—"

"You were the one who pulled over."

"Because you told me to. You were practically out the door before I stopped the car."

My head was shaking as if my reaction was a given. "That poor wolf was hurt!"

"*Wolf*," Jesse echoed. "Do you *hear* yourself? That thing could have attacked you!"

"It looks like it did." Dad frowned, and I twisted and winced as the motion tugged on scratches on my back.

"Ouch, no." I groaned. "That wasn't the wolf, it was something else."

"There was nothing else out there, Tay." Jesse exhaled edgily.

Dad was scrutinising the cuts. "Jess, can you bring in Taylor's things? I'd better get these cleaned up before they get infected."

I shook my head and took a step towards the car. "I'm fine, I can get—"

"Taylor, listen to your father please," Mum said. I sighed and turned to him as he led me into the house. It was almost as if nothing had changed.

*

23

If I wasn't convinced before, now I was utterly sure that *nothing* had changed. My room was still exactly as I left it, my old, oversized clothes still hanging and folded neatly in my cupboard, and last year's calendar still hung over my desk waiting to be replaced.

Dad got his medical bag out and cleaned the scratches on my back, causing them to sting freshly as if he was re-slicing them open with his scalpel. Once Jesse had brought in my luggage, he gave my father a hand, helping him to dress the wound as his medical protégé. For dinner, my mother cooked lasagne, my favourite, and piled it high on my plate. The sight of it frightened me, even after spending a year in Italy, and I only ate enough to be polite, without taking in too many unnecessary calories and claiming my previous bad habits from my prior life.

When dinner was over, I excused myself and headed back to my room to make a start on cleaning out the cupboard of my frumpy, outsized clothes, and replaced them with the few I had acquired on my travels. It was painfully clear to me that I needed to replenish my wardrobe now that I was home since my one pair of fitting jeans that I'd been wearing was now covered in the wolf's blood, and the weather in South Coast was still deciding whether to be winter or summer.

It was beyond my bedtime when I finally finished the clean out, and piled the enormous mountain of clothes by my door, ready for a new owner. I could feel the fatigue weighing heavily on my awareness, and that, along with the dull stinging of my back, told me a decent sleep was definitely on the top of my to-do list. If only I could settle myself.

I slumped in my computer chair and assessed my room. I felt like a foreigner in the surroundings, as if I had woken from a dream that was too real to be fantasy. I wasn't this girl any more, and I never wanted to be her again.

"Hey, Tay," Jesse murmured, knocking on my door lightly as he pushed it open. I spun around on my chair and smiled weakly.

"Hey, Jess."

"Here are your books for this semester," he replied, holding them out towards me. "And I signed you up for all your units. I start my surgical placement at Iris Cove Private Hospital on Monday so I can give you a ride most days. You'll have to find your own way in on Wednesdays because you don't start until ten thirty."

"Thanks." I nodded, glancing at my timetable. The study load for veterinary science wasn't nearly as bad as it was for medicine. I didn't know how Jesse did it. My eyes closed as I kicked myself internally. How could I have forgotten that I wasn't the only one to spend a year away from South Coast this year?

"Oh my God, Jesse, I'm so selfish," I sighed. "How was your internship in Half Moon Bay?"

My brother smiled in understanding. "It was really incredible. I got a lot of priceless experience. It was nothing like a year in Europe, but it was as much fun… for me at least."

I laughed. "You're a nerd."

"Yeah,"

"But you wear it well. When did you get back again?"

"A couple of months now, remember? I finished up at the end of last year, I spent Christmas back here," he replied, and his forehead creased. "I'm sure I wrote it in my emails."

"You probably did." I half shrugged. "My brain is just working at half speed... or not working, I don't know."

Jesse grinned. "Are you settling back in?"

"It's weird. Kind of surreal actually," I sighed tiredly.

Jesse folded his arms and leant against my doorframe. "Why?"

"It's all the same, but I'm different, you know? I feel like I'm stepping back in time into a dream or something."

"You think you've changed that much?"

"It feels like it," I said, tipping my head. "I mean, I guess I'm still the same person. I don't think anyone can change who they really are underneath, but everything feels alien to me now."

Jesse looked up, his grey eyes were sad. "I'm sorry you don't feel like you fit any more."

"That's just it," I sighed. "I never really felt like I fit. I just think now I accept it. I thought that maybe changing what I look like might change that, but it didn't change anything. I don't think I'll ever fit, but maybe that's okay."

"Sure you do, you fit with me. It's us against the world, it always has been."

I smiled. "No, it's always been just you, Jesse. I never fit into your world."

"It's not my world though, Tay. I don't know when you'll realise that." He frowned. "You belong where you choose to belong and, who knows, maybe things will be different now that you are more comfortable in yourself?"

"I love you, Jesse."

"I love you too," he whispered. "Get some sleep. It's been a long day for you, and you've only got tomorrow before classes start back."

I nodded unenthusiastically at the prospect of starting back at uni. "Okay. And hey, thanks for picking me up. I'm sorry about your car. You can use mine until it's fixed."

His eyebrows rose as he nodded, but then his expression turned serious. "You know, next time you might not be so lucky. You could have been hurt a lot worse today."

"I know. I just thought I could help."

"I know, and it's good that you care, but you've got to consider your own safety in some situations," he replied. "And even though I appreciate the practice, I don't want you to always be my patient."

I looked down and smiled. "Granted."

"I'm glad you're home," he sighed. "I really missed you."

I drew in a breath and let it out, glancing up at my brother. "I missed you too, Jess. You're, like, the only person I missed."

"I'm the only person you kept in touch with too." He nodded. "April kept asking how you were going. She said she emailed you, but you didn't respond to her when you were away."

I looked down and thought back to my blonde, former best friend. Former in the sense that there was a time we were inseparable, but before I left, she'd made her feelings perfectly clear on the fact that she thought I was a spoilt little brat who always got what she wanted. She had been slightly bitter that my parents had offered to bankroll my European vacation. What she declined to appreciate though was the fact I had saved enough from my part-time job as a veterinary assistant to pay for myself. I had moonlighted as someone similar in Italy at shelters and such to pay my own way; my parent's money never factored into the equation.

"April and I didn't part on the best of terms," I murmured, twisting my 'Tl' scrabble piece ring around my left middle finger.

"She mentioned she upset you before you left." He nodded. "She said she's sorry."

"I know, I read the emails," I replied, and then yawned. Jesse gave me an understanding smile.

"I'll let you sleep," he whispered, giving me a wink before turning to leave. "Good night, Tay."

"'Night, Jess," I sighed, watching as he left.

I looked back to the Everest of clothes by my door – the first of many mountains I'd need to face now that I was home. It wasn't going to be easy being back. I drummed my fingers on my desk and glanced over to my hand luggage resting against the table leg, which I hadn't yet unpacked. I leant down and unzipped the green leather bag, and frowned at the blood-stained jacket that I'd stuffed in there on the way home. As I pulled it out to add to my washing pile, out tumbled the silver dagger. I picked it off the floor and looked at it properly for the first time. It was long and sleek, with a crescent moon carved into the blade, and at the end of the coiled handle was a milky coloured stone. I turned to my computer and pulled up an internet search, typing in all combinations of white gemstone, crystal, crescent, and ended up finding a page with a stone almost identical to the one on the dagger. A Moonstone.

"Also known as a water opal, fish-eye, and wolf's-eye," I read aloud. Wolf's eye? Was it just a strange coincidence that I found the dagger in the shoulder of a wolf?

I blinked, and nearly nodded off. Any further investigation on the dagger would have to wait until I had gotten more sleep. I wiped the blade clean with the spoiled jacket and dropped it in my desk drawer, before throwing the jacket on the wash pile, and tumbling into my bed. I had barely pulled the covers over me when my eyelids rolled closed.

*

I slept through almost the entire next day, only waking to get a snack for dinner and go for a bit of a run. Since it was Sunday, and late afternoon, no shops were open for me to begin the overhaul of my old life in the form of clothing. So, I just focused on bagging up my existing undesirables and piled them into the back of my small silver four-wheel drive, ready to take to the needy when I had the chance. I couldn't sleep that night, and that frustrated me because I knew that Monday meant I'd have to face concentrating on a new semester of classes on next to no sleep. I tried to make good use of my time by reading over the textbooks for my new units, but after hours of focusing on words that used to make a little more sense to me, I drifted into a dreamless doze. No time seemed to have passed when Jesse nudged me awake from my slumped position at my desk, telling me that classes started in a little over half an hour.

I unenthusiastically rose to my feet and felt my back crack in a few different places, and then fossicked around my room for something to wear. I hadn't had the chance to wash my only pair of jeans, which were still covered with wolf-blood from my failed rescue attempt.

I ended up throwing on a cream dress with a brown spotted print and coupled it with a brown leather belt and ankle boots. On my way out the door, I stopped by my mum's closet and grabbed one of her leather jackets to top it off. Thankfully, I was her size now. My mother grew up a ballet dancer, so staying in shape was always a priority for her.

I grabbed an apple and met Jesse out the front, already waiting in my car to drive us to South Coast University. It barely registered to me that his car was still out of action, but it didn't make a difference whether we took my car or his. I actually preferred the protection of my four-wheel drive, but there was no doubt more style in a Mercedes convertible.

"Hey, Jesse, I thought that was you. What are you doing here? Why are you driving your sister's car?" a voice called from across the one-way street as Jesse shifted into park. I climbed out and walked around to where my brother stood.

"Hey, who's your friend?" Brandon continued, walking across to us. His eyebrows rose at me, and a smile crept onto his face. His light blue eyes were practically glowing as he extended his hand towards me. "Hi there, I'm Brandon."

I caught my breath at the close proximity and then felt my expression harden. Jesse's eyebrows pulled together as he glanced at me before returning the look to his friend.

"Are you serious, bro?" Jesse asked incredulously. "Don't be an idiot, you've met her."

Brandon tipped his head. "No, I'd remember someone this beautiful."

I forced a smile. "Apparently not."

"It's my sister." Jesse groaned. "So quit trying to hit on her."

"Taylor?" Brandon repeated in a voice that was both confused and appalled. "No, your sister Taylor is—" He stopped and feigned a smile as my eyebrows lifted and my head fell curiously to the side. Brandon laughed nervously. "Wow, you look great. I mean, Europe really agreed with you…"

"Save it," Jesse sighed. "Listen, I need to get to work. Will you be okay from here?"

I drew in a breath and let it out. "Yes, I'll be fine. Thanks for the lift."

Jesse glanced to Brandon, who still appeared to be in shock. He leant over and hit him lightly in the chest with the back of his hand, which seemed to snap him out of it.

31

"Behave," Jesse warned Brandon, opening the car door, and sliding back behind the wheel. He turned his attention to me and smiled weakly. "I'll meet you back here at four thirty."

"Four-thirty." I nodded, glancing at my bare wrist. Great. I'd forgotten a watch. I patted my pockets and fished out my phone, pointing at the display. "Okay."

"Have a good day, you two." He laughed, starting the engine. I watched him go, and smiled, lifting a hand to wave. I let out a sigh once my car disappeared, and turned towards the university building. Brandon defrosted and walked to my side.

"So, where's your first class?" he asked.

I looked up at him. "What are you doing?"

Brandon looked to the side. "I don't get it."

"Jesse's gone, you don't have to talk to me," I replied awkwardly. It was the longest time he'd spent alone in my presence since we were thirteen, and then it had been under just as awkward circumstances. I had been borderline obsessed with him, and after years of pining from afar, I mustered up the courage to ask him out. He'd never given me an answer, but the echo of his laughter haunted my nightmares for a long time. I'd never told Jesse. I was too ashamed.

"Maybe I want to talk to you." He shrugged.

I looked at him incredulously and then started walking up the road to where my first class was. "When have you ever wanted to talk to me?"

He paused for a moment, and then jogged after me. He was your typical physiotherapy student. "So I can't start? How was Europe?"

32

"Aren't you going to be late for class?" I asked. I hated the fact that my heart rate responded to his presence.

"They don't start until ten thirty."

"So why are you here so early?"

"Nostalgia. It's my last semester." He shrugged. "So, Europe, huh? I suppose you know I spent a year and a half travelling after school finished; before I started to study."

"Yes, I know. You've been Jesse's best friend since we were twelve," I sighed, pushing open the door to the block of classes.

"Taylor, wait," he replied, grabbing my hand. As he did, I gasped, letting my bag slip from my shoulder. The contents tumbled out all over the floor.

Brandon shook his head. "Oh, geez, I'm so—"

"Just go, Brandon," I mumbled, lowering to gather my stuff. "I don't need your help."

Brandon exhaled and left while I began jamming the last couple of things into my bag.

"Excuse me, miss?" a honey-smooth voice said.

His accent threw me because it was English, but mixed with something else –was it French? I could have sworn it was French, or maybe I just missed Europe. I looked up, still in a fluster and then thawed at the sight of the guy with sepia-coloured hair kneeling beside me. I blinked and looked down to what he was extending towards me.

"You dropped this," he noted, gesturing towards my student identification card. Yes, it was definitely French mixed with his English accent. I hesitated and frowned at the photo of my former self. It was practically a slap in the face.

"Taylor Mistry," he murmured. "You wouldn't want to lose your identity."

As much as I wanted to snatch the card from him and run and hide, I couldn't move. It was almost an effort to breathe. The stranger smiled, and his olive green eyes lowered as he tucked the card into my open bag.

I opened my mouth to say thank you, or something, but he stood in one movement and then disappeared as quickly as he had appeared.

Phase Two
The Darkest Black

"Taylor Mistry," the library clerk mused. He scrutinised my student card as if it was a fake ID, and I was trying to get into a club.

"Well, I've got to say... your photo does not do you justice," he said with a grin, handing it back. I snatched it from him and sighed as I headed towards the exit with my giant stack of secondary reading books.

My day had only gotten weirder since my mysterious encounter with the green-eyed stranger this morning, or rather, since I'd arrived here and Brandon chased me down the street. For the entire day, I felt as though I was being watched, only, not in the sense that I had been expecting. I mean, sure, I guess I noticed the odd head turning my way, but that didn't really register to me, not as much as the unnerving notion that another pair of eyes were on me – a hidden pair that I couldn't quite explain or rationally describe.

"Tay! You're back!" a shrill, familiar voice screeched from behind me as I stopped by the curb to wait for Jesse to arrive. I half turned to see April and nodded.

"Hey, April."

"Hol-ly *cow*," she gasped. "*Look at you*! You're so *skinny*."

I feigned a smile, and looked impatiently up the street, almost willing Jesse to come. *Now*.

"You're not still in a mood with me because of what I said before you left, are you?" she asked, folding her arms across her chest. "I mean, way to hold a grudge."

"I'm not in a mood." I shrugged half-heartedly. "Actually, April, I'm just not in *the* mood right now."

She rolled her eyes. "Right, because now you look good, you don't need friends."

I swivelled to stare at her. "What?"

"I know how it is," she sighed.

"You don't know anything."

I stepped out on the road and then shrieked as the strap of my bag pulled me backwards. A car breezed past me, and the wheel narrowly missed my foot.

"Do you have a death wish?" April shouted, releasing her grip on my bag. I frowned since it was the second time since I'd been back that someone had asked me that.

"Thanks," I breathed. "That car just came out of nowhere."

She shook her head. "You should be more careful. Clearly you're fading away, so drivers can't even see *you* any more."

I couldn't help but laugh at the serious tone in her voice. "Okay."

"Hey, Taylor, you ready?" Jesse called from the street. I glanced over my shoulder and saw that he was causing a traffic jam.

"Thanks again," I said to April. "And, hey, we should do coffee or something. I've got so much to tell you."

She nodded. "I'd like that."

Jesse beeped the horn. "Tay!"

"See you," I waved, checking both ways of the one-way road before I darted across into the car.

"Hey, sorry," I sighed. "I was expecting you earlier."

Jesse glanced at his watch. "I'm sorry I'm late. Was that April you were talking to?"

"Yes."

"All good?"

"Kind of."

"Did I hear you ask her to catch up?" he asked.

"Yeah." I shrugged. "I figured I should."

He laughed. "Sound more enthusiastic, Tay."

I frowned. "She said now that since I look good, I don't think I need friends."

"She said that?"

"You don't think she's right, do you?"

Jesse pulled a face. "Of course not. Don't listen to her; she's just bitter and lonely. Besides, you've always looked good."

I rolled my eyes. "Right."

"It's true." He smiled. "So, Brandon didn't bother you too much this morning, did he?"

"Brandon." I groaned. "He… he's…"

"I know." He chuckled. "Consider it a compliment."

"A compliment that he didn't notice me before but now he's all for talking?" I asked.

Jesse tipped his head. "It's not him wanting to talk to you that concerns me."

I laughed. "Don't be silly. He's not interested in me."

Jesse smirked as he pulled up our driveway. "Just be careful. You seem to be getting a little more attention now, and not all guys have honourable intentions."

"Relax, Jess," I said. "I don't take any of it seriously. I actually find it funny. Who would think me attractive?"

"You really don't see yourself clearly, Taylor. I'm not sure you ever have."

"You have to say that because you're my brother."

He rolled his eyes and opened his car door. "It's because I'm your brother that I don't have to say that."

"Hey, Jess," I said. "I might go to the shops to try to buy some clothes that fit."

"Okay," he replied and threw me the keys.

"You don't want to come, do you?"

"No, thanks." He smiled. "Unless you *want* me to."

I laughed. "It's fine, I wouldn't subject you to that."

"Well, just take care driving. You're probably not used to it," he replied. "I've got to meet Ashley anyway."

I pulled a face. "Is she still around?"

"Don't start please," he sighed. "You've made your feelings on my girlfriend perfectly clear."

"Girlfriend. She's so horrible."

"Okay." He nodded. "Have fun."

I slid into the driver's seat, and slowly went through the motions. Seatbelt, keys in the ignition, engine on, foot on brake, hand brake off, shift into gear. Jesse waited to make sure I could operate it properly before backing towards the house. I wasn't sure whether to be offended or thankful.

*

Shopping for clothes was about as unpleasant as I expected. Although I had more of a selection of nice things, I still hated trying them on as much as I had before. So, I stuck to the essentials: jeans, a couple of tops, a sweater, a coat, a winter dress.

After a couple of hours, my shoulder began to ache, and I was also tired and ready for bed again.

The downside to South Coast was that it was quite a small city, but it took me longer than it should have to get back to my car. I seemed to be haunted by people from my past and walked around long ways to dodge the ghosts from high school. I wasn't ready to face them yet. Regardless, those hidden eyes that I'd I felt on campus still felt like they were fixated on me like I was stuck in crosshairs. It was unnerving, and when I got back to my car, it was a welcome refuge.

I collected myself for a moment, taking a few deep breaths, and then went to start it. The engine revved, strained, and then cut out. I tried again and the same thing happened. I didn't have the faintest idea about cars, so I knew I wouldn't be much help, but I got out anyway and popped the hood. I didn't know what I was supposed to be looking for, but it all seemed fine to me.

"Why won't you work?" I mumbled as I ran my fingers over the metal parts. I took a step back and looked around. No one was about to ask, so I pulled out my phone to call someone. But who would I call? Jesse didn't have a car, and I was pretty sure my dad would still be at work. There was Mum, but she didn't know much more than me, and I didn't want to deal with a mechanic. I bit my lower lip and then heard a rustling in the bushes that made me jump. I closed the hood and climbed back into the car, deciding to call Jesse so at least he could send help.

"We're on our way," Jesse said. "Stay inside the car."

"We?" I asked and then groaned internally. He and Ashley.

"Don't start, Taylor," he replied.

"Okay," I sighed. "Thanks."

I rested my head back and looked out at the darkening surroundings. It was just past twilight, and the pretty bluish hues were turning to black. I wasn't afraid of the dark, I'd never had a reason to be, but there was something about the empty parking lot that made me feel unsafe. Maybe it was the unseen eyes that I felt, or perhaps it was the fact I knew that I was stranded. Regardless, the sooner Jesse and Ashley arrived, the better.

"You are proving to be much more trouble than I remember, sis," Jesse said as Ashley's car pulled up ten minutes later. It felt like a long ten minutes.

"I know. I'm obviously jinxed," I answered. "Can you fix it?"

"He can't, but I can," Brandon chimed in. My head snapped around to see him clambering out of Ashley's back seat.

"Oh," I sighed. "You."

"Hello again." Brandon grinned. "What seems to be the problem?"

"It won't start," I replied flatly.

"Taylor." Jesse groaned.

I rolled my eyes. "It just revs but doesn't catch. It sounds sort of sick."

"Let me have a look-see," Brandon said. He slid in the driver's seat and turned the key. The car made the same choking sound it had previously.

"Why did you bring him, Jesse?" I whispered.

"I might be a surgeon, but he is a car surgeon," Jesse answered. "He knows more about this stuff than me."

I folded my arms and looked over at Ashley as she fell by Jesse's side. I'd almost forgotten she was here too.

"Hello, Taylor," she said almost reluctantly.

Jesse elbowed me.

"Hi, Ashley," I replied. "How are you?"

Her brown eyes glowed in the streetlight. "Good thanks. You?"

"Fine." I nodded. Jesse's arm pulled her close to his side, and I looked at Brandon who sounded as if he was torturing my car.

41

"It's the battery," he said. "Jesse, can you get those cables for me? It just needs a jumpstart."

Jesse stepped away to help Brandon, leaving Ashley and me alone. She was quite attractive in an obvious sort of way. She had a pretty face, shoulder-length red hair, but was plain without the aid of makeup. She was quite slender with curves in all the right places, and the type of girl who had received attention from boys from early adolescence, so was never single for long. In other words, the complete opposite of me.

"How was Europe?" she asked. It sounded as if it was more to fill the silence than out of actual interest.

"It was great." I nodded. "How's, uh, what were you doing with yourself again?"

"Beauty therapy," she answered. "And good thanks."

Of course, beauty therapy. How could I forget?

"Ash, can you move your car a bit closer?" Brandon called. Ashley stepped away quickly, clearly relieved for the distraction. I stood back just in case she got any ideas to run me over. I'd had quite enough near-death experiences in the last few days.

*

Brandon got the car started with a jumpstart in next to no time, and Jesse rode back with me while Ashley gave Brandon a lift home. Ashley didn't seem pleased at the suggestion, but it made the most sense. I think she was annoyed that I had disrupted their evening – as if I had somehow planned it.

42

"Thanks for coming out," I murmured when we arrived home. "I really appreciate it."

"That's okay," he replied, putting my keys on the table.

I looked down. He seemed to be a little upset with me.

"I'm sorry I ruined your night," I continued. "I didn't mean—"

"It's okay, Taylor," he interrupted. "It's not your fault."

"Okay. I am trying you know."

"Trying?"

"To settle back in," I said. "It's just harder than I thought it would be."

"I know you are," he answered. "But what's that got to do with anything?"

I shrugged. "I just wanted you to know it."

"I do. Have you eaten?"

"I'm not hungry."

"You shouldn't skip meals."

I laughed. "I know."

"Sorry," he murmured, walking to the fridge.

"Hey, Jesse?"

"Mm?"

I bit my lip. "Let's move out together."

He looked up from the open fridge. "What?"

"I can't be here... surrounded by all these depressing memories of my old life," I answered.

Jesse shook his head. "Tay, your old life wasn't that bad—"

"Regardless," I sighed. "What do you think? You and me? We could get a place close to Iris Cove Private Hospital, so you wouldn't even need to drive to work."

He smiled. "You just want your car back."

"I just want my brother back." I shrugged. "Besides, we're twenty-three this year. It's about time we flew from the nest."

He looked to the side thoughtfully.

I drew in a deep breath. "What do you say?"

"Yeah." He smiled. "Okay, let's do it."

Phase Three
The Tooth Pendant

"Is this seat taken?" Brandon asked on Friday. It was the early afternoon and I had finished my classes for the day. I was waiting in the university common room, drawing circles in my natural yogurt with the red plastic spoon.

"No." I shrugged.

"Do you mind if I sit?" he continued, stepping onto the bench. He was already seated before I could answer.

"Please," I murmured a little sarcastically.

Brandon smiled. "So how's your week been?"

It still confused me to have him speaking directly to me. For as long as I can remember, Brandon avoided this at all cost. I even remember him once asking Jesse to tell me something when I was sitting right beside him.

"Fine." I shrugged. "I mean, it's still weird being back."

"For sure." He nodded. "So, Jesse mentioned you guys are getting a place together. That's pretty cool."

"Yeah."

"He said you found one close to the hospital that your mum used to rent when she first got here."

"Yep."

"So when do you move in?" he asked.

I shrugged. "You seem to know more about this than I do."

He chuckled. "Right."

I pushed the yogurt to the side.

"So, are you going to the back to uni party tonight?" he asked. His pale blue eyes unnerved me the way they looked over my face. I felt like I was thirteen again, catching my breath at the sight of him. Regardless of how badly he treated me, and despite the fact he dated every other girl in our year but didn't look twice at me, I still found my resolve wavering as those eyes bore into mine. He was gorgeous but he knew it, and yet, I was a goner. Apparently the torch I held for him wasn't easily extinguished.

"I wasn't planning on it," I answered slowly. "I have, um, work this afternoon, and some reading to do."

His eyebrow lifted. "Work?"

"Yeah, I have a part-time position helping out at the vet clinic near Iris Cove Hospital," I replied. "It's not that flash, but it's all experience."

"For sure, for sure." He nodded. "That's pretty cool though."

"Yeah."

"So when does work finish?"

I inhaled. Jesse's car was fixed now, but he still dropped me in so I could save on parking. "Well, it depends on when I can get there. I said I'd try and put in four or five hours, so could be late since Jesse doesn't finish until—"

"I can drop you," he said, sticking his finger in my yogurt. He pulled a face. "That is terrible."

"It's natural," I replied.

His nose wrinkled. "Ugh. So how about it?"

"How about what?" I asked. I was a little distracted that he still managed to look good even when disgusted.

"I can take you to work, so you can finish earlier and come tonight," he replied.

"No, that's fine," I sighed. "I still have reading to do for my classes anyway."

He scoffed. "Reading? Who does that at all, never mind on a Friday night?"

"I don't want to fail."

"Okay, so you have the whole weekend to do it." He shrugged. "Come on, live a little. Come."

I shook my head. "I don't... I don't know."

"Jesse will come," he said. "And Ashley."

I pulled a face.

He laughed. "Come on. Please, Taylor."

I felt my determination weaken further at the sound of my name as it lingered on his tongue.

"Maybe... if Jesse comes," I replied.

"Awesome." He grinned, standing up. "Are you coming then?"

I blinked. "Coming where?"

"Work." He chuckled. "Remember?"

I shook my head incredulously. "Right."

*

I wasn't quite sure what to make of it, but I was beginning to think that I had made it all up. There was no way that this Brandon could have ever been so unpleasant towards me when he seemed so genuine, so sweet, and so obliging. He dropped me at the vet and offered to call Jesse to tell him that I didn't need collecting from uni. Then he offered to give me a lift whenever I finished. That, however, I respectfully declined. But it was still quite bizarre.

After work, Jesse picked me up and took me home to make myself presentable for the back to uni party. Apparently it was at a club across the park and esplanade from the university campus. I hadn't been there before, but Jesse and Brandon were familiar with the place since they were more sociable than I am, or was.

When we arrived, April was already there. She greeted me warmly, throwing her arms around me as if no time had passed or no rift had been created by my absence. April and I had been friends since high school, and apparently, that stood for something. I was just glad that I knew someone else here. Brandon arrived shortly after Jesse and me, and he was flanked by Ashley who seemed hell-bent on monopolising my brother's time. This might not have otherwise bothered me, but April was a little preoccupied with demanding attention from every guy in the room, and Brandon, despite the turnaround, was lapping up the attention of the other girls there.

"Dance with me," he eventually whispered in my ear, sending goose-bumps down my body. He pulled back and smiled, and his eyes were glowing.

"I don't know…" I started, but it was no use. He had already taken my hand and pulled me against him. His arms locked around me, and my heart flipped with the closeness. I wasn't used to it, especially not from him. Leo had been the only guy to break through my defensive walls, and even then, it was handholding and the odd kiss. He appreciated my need to move at my own pace considering this was all new to me.

However, Brandon was different. At first, I thought I liked it. I enjoyed that he had chosen me out of all the pretty, brainless girls that threw themselves at him, until I realised that I wasn't that special. I felt like an accessory being at his side, the way he acted, and the way he flaunted me felt like he was showing off a shiny new toy. I felt alone, a different kind of alone to why I used to feel when I was invisible. This kind of loneliness was the kind that came with being surrounded by people who didn't care what you had to say; the kind that I might as well have been invisible for. At least before I knew who my friends were.

The walls in the club felt like they were closing in on me, and when I could, I broke away and slipped out the front to get some air. I didn't know where I was going, but I knew that I needed to be away from people. I headed straight towards the darkened park, knowing it was probably a stupid idea, but I didn't care. I just needed to breathe.

It worked.

After a few minutes of sitting under the protection of a willow tree, the clouds in my head began to clear. I started to remember who I was, and what I stood for. Away from Brandon, I could see how easy it was for me to be sucked into the faux acceptance of the pretty people. But that wasn't me. It never would be.

"You don't look like you are having much fun," a phantom voice said – a French-inflected, English accent. I jumped and looked around the shadows, then saw two glowing olive-green coloured eyes staring back at me.

A beat later, he dropped into the light, and I made out his face and the dark features that complimented his beautiful teak-coloured skin against his light auburn hair. His perfectly shaped lips stretched into a smile as he appraised my surprised expression.

I looked down shyly, before quickly returning my gaze to his hypnotic stare.

"No, I guess I'm not," I answered.

He nodded. "You are Taylor, right? Taylor Mistry."

I nodded in silent reply, feeling a little guilty that I couldn't return the familiarity. "I'm sorry. I don't know your name."

"Don't be. I don't believe I ever gave it to you," he said, and his smile broadened. His teeth were perfect and pearly white. They seemed to glow in the moonlight. "I'm Harper Lovett."

"Harper," I murmured. "What are you doing out here?"

"Same as you, I suppose." He shrugged in the darkness. "Just getting some air; enjoying the night."

I pressed my lips together. "I don't remember seeing you inside."

"I guess I'm more of an outsider."

I smiled. "So, what's your story then? You don't like people or something?"

He chuckled. "I'm not a misanthrope or anything. I guess I just prefer my own company."

"I know what you mean."

He tipped his head. "You don't strike me as the kind of person who knows what it's like to be alone."

"Maybe not alone, but I know what it's like to feel lonely," I answered. "Sometimes being surrounded by people is the loneliest place on earth, especially if they look right through you as if you're not there."

Harper frowned. "I don't understand how anyone can overlook you."

"Maybe not now," I mumbled. "But I didn't always look this way."

"I know what you used to look like, and my point remains."

I felt my forehead crease in confusion. "How do you know what I used to look like?"

"I saw your student ID card," he replied. Comprehension took a few beats to hit.

"Right... you stopped to help me the other day when I dropped my bag."

"Right."

I smiled weakly and stared at the only person that seemed to notice me when I was invisible, and was able to free me from my deepest fears and inner thoughts. I would have felt self-conscious, but I felt a strange sense of instantaneous trust with him that was otherwise uncommon with me. His light green eyes penetrated mine, drawing me into their trance. There was a certain kind of sadness to them as if maybe he had spent a lifetime alone. I felt the sudden urge to throw my arms around him and hug him until all that sadness melted away.

"Well, you don't strike me as the kind of person that likes to spend all his time alone either," I said after a stretch of comfortable silence had passed between us.

He smiled a kind of secret smile and then laughed. His eyes traced to the starlit sky, and I didn't quite understand the joke. When his smile faded, his face hardened.

"I should go," he whispered.

I felt a strange sense of desperation, like maybe he was saying goodbye forever. "Do you have to?"

He nodded, resigned. "It was very nice to meet you, Taylor."

"You too, Harper," I answered honestly.

A shadow of a smile tugged at the corner of his lips as he turned to leave, and before I knew what I was doing, I jumped up.

"Wait, can I see you again?" I asked.

Harper half turned, his expression almost torn.

"I'm not sure if that's a good idea," he said slowly. I felt my face drop from the rejection, and my formerly insecure self bubbled to the surface. At least there was no laughter this time.

"Oh." I frowned.

"No, I mean…" He stopped and sighed, shaking his head. "It's not you, I… I…"

I shook my head and took a step back. "It's fine, you don't have to explain. I just… it was nice to talk to you, that's all."

"No, Taylor, wait." He exhaled, still conflicted in his tone. "I mean it, it's *not* you. I would see you, but…"

"You're not making much sense."

"I know, it's just a little hard to explain."

I turned. "Don't bother, I get it."

"You get what?" he asked.

I paused and glanced over my shoulder.

"You're a lone wolf, right?" I said.

"Lone wolf?"

"You don't need people. That's okay. I used to be like that too," I replied. "But, if you ever change your mind and decide you need someone…"

"Taylor?" Brandon's voice called. "Are you out here?"

Harper's eyes lifted in the direction the voice had come, and I turned to follow his eye line. When I spun back, the place he'd been standing was empty, and he was nowhere to be seen. It was as if he'd vanished – melted into the shadows of the moonlit night.

"There you are, where'd you go?" Brandon asked, making me jump as he suddenly appeared at my side.

53

"I just… needed some air," I sighed, still searching for any trace that Harper had been there, and I hadn't just been talking to myself.

"Come on, April's buying everyone jelly shots," he said, towing me back towards the direction of the neon lights. My eyes caught sight of something glinting in the dirt, and I pulled away from his hold.

"I'll meet you back there in a minute. I just… I need a few more seconds here," I answered. "I promise."

He looked at me for a moment and then shrugged. "Okay."

"Okay." I nodded, waiting for him to leave. He stepped away a little unsurely, and then headed back, glancing once over his shoulder as if questioning my sanity. I didn't care. I hastened towards the glimmering jewel that was in the place where Harper had been and then I checked around me before lowering to the ground where a tooth that had been turned into a pendant lay. It looked as if it had belonged to a large earth-dwelling animal – definitely not the kind of shark tooth I'd seen surfers wear. I would have guessed that it had belonged to a lion or a large dog. I heard a rustling, and glanced around, then straightened quickly and headed back towards the crowded club. Back to where the cookie-cutter people swayed back and forth mindlessly.

"Is everything okay?" Brandon whispered into my ear after throwing back a shot. His breath was warm, sweet, and sent a shiver down my spine.

I nodded in reply.

"You sure?" he pressed, brushing the back of his fingers lightly over my cheek. I flinched at his touch, and his brows drew.

"I'm fine," I answered before he could question me further. "Just tired."

His baby blue eyes glistened. "I can give you a ride home if you like?"

My heart squeezed nervously. "I think I'll just wait for Jesse."

I looked around and spotted him at the same time Brandon must have. He was with Ashley, quite occupied, and didn't appear to want his sister as company any time soon. I looked back to Brandon and forced a smile.

"Are you sure you want to be a third wheel with those two?" he asked over the thumping music. I panned the room, trying to find April to ask her for a ride, and spotted her on the dance floor surrounded by a crowd of guys. Typical. Some people were reliably unreliable.

"I can catch an Uber." I shrugged. "I don't want to ruin your night."

His hand found its way to my lower back. "You're not ruining anything."

"Are you sure?" I frowned. I wasn't sure whether I wanted him to agree or disagree. I wasn't sure whether I wanted his attention, or whether this was all just a terrible idea. Regardless, I needed to get home somehow, and he was increasingly looking like my best option.

"Absolutely." He smiled.

"Okay, I'll just let Jesse know that we're leaving."

His hand moved up my back. "Okay."

I stepped quickly over to my brother and tapped his shoulder. "Jesse."

He pulled away from Ashley, who took a breath of air as if she'd been underwater for too long. Jesse seemed a little disoriented.

"Taylor," he said. "What's up?"

"So, I'm going to go," I sighed, glancing at Ashley who was shooting me daggers with her eyes. "Um, Brandon's going to drop me home."

"Brandon?" Jesse repeated. "Is he okay to drive? He's been drinking."

I looked over at him and shrugged. "Guess so."

"Taylor…"

"Well, I want to go, and unless you do too… which I'm guessing you don't," I replied. "I'll be fine. It's not that far."

Jesse thought for a moment.

"I don't like it," he said finally.

"Jesse, she said she'll be fine." Ashley exhaled as her fingers drew circles on his forearms. "Brandon will look after her."

Jesse glanced at her and sighed, turning back to me. "Text me when you get home, and if you think he's over the limit, you drive his car back and get him to crash on the couch. Okay?"

"Yes, Dad." I groaned.

"I'm serious, Taylor, this isn't Europe," he warned. "It's your safety I'm worried about."

"Right," I answered. "I'll text you when I'm home."

He nodded and I patted his shoulder before returning to where Brandon was waiting.

"All good?" Brandon smiled.

"Yeah, you know Jesse – ever the worrier," I replied.

He chuckled. "Let's get out of here."

His hand returned to my lower back as he led me from the crowded club. The music and chattering seeming louder when my attention wasn't focused on one voice in particular. When we got outside, it seemed to vanish into the night. My ears rang as the silence took over. I breathed in a gulp of fresh air.

"I'm over here," he said, gesturing to his silver ute. It seemed a bit redundant to me that he drove one. I had never seen him require the services of the tray before. I didn't know what the appeal was.

"Are you sure you're okay to drive?" I asked. "I haven't had anything to drink if you wanted me to."

He smiled. "It takes more than that to send me over the limit."

"If you say so." I shrugged.

"I do," he answered as we reached the car. "It's open."

I headed around to the passenger side and opened the door. Even the interior seemed small. Clean, but small. It was half a car, for no reason.

"So did you have fun tonight?" he asked.

I clipped on my seatbelt. "Sure, it was fine."

Fine. The word seemed to be losing meaning.

"I'm glad you decided to come. I don't know why you haven't before."

I glanced over at him, wondering if that was a legitimate question. Had he even noticed before?

"I never saw the point," I replied. "Clubs aren't really my scene."

He smiled. "So what is your scene then?"

"I prefer quieter places – movie nights, small gatherings, you know. Clubs are too noisy, and a bit too full-on for me."

"You looked like you were having fun," Brandon answered. The car swerved, but he corrected it quickly. I rested my hand on the door.

"Like I said, it was fine," I sighed.

He smirked and turned back to focus on the road. I relaxed a little.

"You're a tough girl to impress," he said. "I don't normally have to try so much."

I felt my forehead crease. "Why?"

"Why what?"

"Why are you trying to impress me?" I asked. The concept seemed stupid to me. In fact, it didn't make sense.

"I thought that would be obvious," he answered, glancing over to smile. I turned my eyes forward, hoping that he'd mirror the motion since I was nervous enough with him driving under the influence without him trying to dazzle me with his charm while he did it.

"Not to me," I said. "I've always been the same person I am now. You wouldn't have to try so hard if you bothered to get to know me before now."

He chuckled. "Maybe I was a little caught up with myself to notice before."

"Maybe."

I knew it had more to do with me being overweight to even rank a mention on his radar.

The short silence between was suddenly interrupted with a loud *bang* that made my breath catch in my throat. The car swerved to the side of the road as Brandon cursed under his breath.

"What was that?" I gasped.

"Flat," he murmured. "And I'm pretty sure my spare is punctured."

I exhaled. "Great."

"Damn, this is going to spoil my rims."

I rolled my eyes and opened the door, preparing to walk the rest of my short journey home. It was only about twenty minutes home at an ambling pace.

"Where are you going?" Brandon called after me.

"Home."

"You're walking? Do you have a death wish?" he asked.

I sighed. "I wish people would stop asking me that."

"What?"

"Nothing. You know, it's not that far."

"But it's dark."

I laughed. "It's night."

"You can't walk home alone, it's not safe," he yelled.

"It's South Coast." I turned and shrugged. "How bad can it be?"

He folded his arms.

"Well, walk with me," I exhaled. "Unless you're planning on sleeping here."

Brandon paused long enough to enable me to turn and make a start to my walking. There was a rustling in the bushes, and I glanced over. I gave a double take at the burning gold eyes that stared back at me. My mouth opened to scream...

"Wait," Brandon called. "I'm coming."

I looked back at him with my mouth still open, and then glanced back to the eyes, but they were gone. I turned back as Brandon jogged over to where I stood.

"I don't remember you being this pushy," he said with amusement.

"I'm surprised you remember me at all," I answered.

"Was I really that horrible to you, or did you just pay more attention to me than other people?"

I blinked and felt my heart rise to my throat. "What do you, uh, mean?"

He shrugged. "I remember the way you used to stare at me."

I cleared my throat and felt my cheeks burn. "You remember that?"

"Yeah." He laughed.

"I'm glad you find it amusing," I frowned, feeling my heart drop to my feet. Regardless of how much I had changed physically, the humiliation of being laughed at still cut me deeper than any knife could reach.

"Sorry, I'm not laughing at you," he said.

"Right."

"Hey," he sighed, catching my hand. "I'm sorry. It was actually kind of flattering."

"Kind of."

"I don't know if you noticed, but I was a bit of an idiot back then."

"Back then?" I asked, and then couldn't help but laugh. "Yeah, I noticed."

He chuckled. "Okay, I deserved that."

We walked in silence for a few minutes, just the sound of our tread and the rustling of leaves. I had started to find the sound comforting like it was a sign of guardianship rather than being trailed.

"So, tell me about Europe," Brandon said after a few more minutes. We were almost back at my parents' house now.

I looked up. "It was great. Life-changing."

"Look-changing and life-changing." He smiled. "So what was so life-changing about it?"

"The look-changing," I answered. "And I got to see so much and experience things I'd never dreamed. I helped out in a lot of animal shelters, and stayed with locals, it was really incredible."

"Sounds it." He nodded. "And romance?"

"There wasn't a lot of time for romance," I murmured. "I did meet someone on the second last day I was there, but… such is fate."

He shrugged. "There'll be others. Guys will be lining up to be with you. I'm sure they already are."

"Not really."

"So you're telling me that I have no competition?"

I pressed my lips together. I wasn't sure what I was supposed to say, or what was supposed to happen. All I knew was that to Brandon, pursuing girls was a game, and in this case, I was a trophy. The fact that Jesse had provided him with an obstacle had made the game a lot sweeter.

"You're different," he said. I almost forgot that he had asked a question that I hadn't answered yet.

"Different?" I frowned. "How?"

"Than the others. Most girls wouldn't make me work so hard to impress them."

I sighed. "You forget that I'm not most girls. I've known you for almost eleven years, so I know how you operate."

He recoiled. "And how exactly do I operate?"

"I just mean that I know you," I replied. "And I know that you hardly need to work hard to impress the other girls. They swoon over you regardless."

"Right, right." He chuckled. "Other girls swoon, but not you?"

I shrugged. "Maybe once I did."

"But not now?"

"I think if you have to try too hard to impress someone, it's not meant to be," I answered. "I wouldn't want someone to just be with me because I wanted them to. I want them to want me, and to want to be with me. For me."

I had almost forgotten that he was there, forgotten that he was privy to my internal, heartfelt musings. I felt a blush tickle my cheeks when the awareness eventually sunk in.

"I think everyone wants that," Brandon replied thoughtfully. "So that's why you're refusing me? Because I didn't notice you before, so you think that means it's too hard now?"

"You didn't notice me before, and nothing has changed now except the size of my jeans," I said. "Which leads me to believe that you are only interested because I look different, not because you like my personality."

His eyebrows lifted. "That's a little rich coming from you."

"Excuse me?"

"You just said that you knew I was an idiot back in the day, yet you still had a crush on me. Why is that I wonder?" he asked. "Is it because you have a soft spot for idiots, or because of the way *I* look?"

I opened my mouth, but no words came out. Brandon's brow lifted. He was right, and he knew it. I let my jaw return to position and faced forward towards my house as we made our way up the drive.

"I'm just asking you to give me a chance, Taylor," Brandon said as I stepped in front to unlock the door. "Give me the chance that I didn't give you."

I shook my head. "Why should I?"

"Aren't you the least bit curious?"

"Curiosity? Is that a good enough reason to be with someone?"

He tipped his head and wove his fingers through mine. "Is stubbornness a good enough reason to not?"

I breathed a laugh.

"So?" he asked, giving my hand a tug towards him. "What do you say?"

I caught my breath, looking into the crystal blue eyes of the guy I'd had a crush on for as long as I could remember. Listening to how he wanted me and wanted me to take a chance on him. A large part of me was wondering why I was just standing there, delaying the inevitable kiss that sealed the agreement. But then, there was that smaller part that screamed at me to remember that nothing really had changed, and he probably wouldn't be saying these things to me if I'd have come back from Europe looking how I did when I left.

But where did you draw the line? How much could you question people's motives? Why not take chances as they presented themselves? At some point, you needed to just stop thinking and start trusting in yourself. Isn't that what I learnt in my time away? To let people in, and let them love me?

Brandon's fingers rose to my chin, and his thumb brushed over my lips.

I closed my eyes to block the distractions so I could finish thinking through the choice in front of me. But as my world went dark, his thumb fell away, and his lips took its place. All logical thought left my mind.

*

Brandon was asleep on the couch, but I didn't sleep at all. I couldn't seem to close my eyes just in case his lips ended up on mine again. I didn't know what to do when that happened. It was awkward enough the first time. I wasn't equipped for Brandon's intensity or experience. When his arms locked around me, all I wanted to do was run. It didn't make sense.

"What's wrong?" Brandon asked as he pulled back and scrutinised my face. I wasn't sure what expression he found; only that it was frozen on. *"Taylor?"*

I blinked. *"Yes?"*

"Yes?" he said. *"Is that your answer to my earlier question, or are you just answering to your name?"*

My forehead creased, my head was empty. *"What?"*

"My question... your name?"

"Did you ask me my name?" I asked dumbly, and then clapped my hand to my forehead. *"Your question, right, about giving you a chance."*

He smiled and it was sympathetic. It was a smile that I knew too well.

I shook my head. *"I just need to think. Can I have time to think?"*

"Sure," he answered. *"Well, you're home so I'll—"*

"No, stay. Jesse said you should stay. You can have the couch. You don't have a car."

Brandon pressed his lips together. Disappointment… another emotion I recognised well.

"Thanks."

Nothing much was said after that. A few pleasantries while I made up a bed for him, a couple of mumblings about how my dad was working late, and Mum was probably already asleep. We said a polite good night, and here I was lying awake while Brandon slept in the next room. I knew he was sleeping because I could hear his slow, even breaths. I could also hear the vague scratching of branches on my window, and the creaks and cracks of the floorboards, of the furniture, of the shadows.

I don't know when it happened, but at some point, I managed to fall asleep. I only know this because the next thing I knew, I was waking up and it was morning. As the memories flooded back, my heart whipped into a sprint. Brandon's car got a flat tyre, he walked me home, he kissed me, he was in the next room, and he was waiting for an answer. Brandon wanted me to take a chance on him. But what did that mean? Did he want to date me, or something else? What did I want from him? I still didn't know. A part of me wanted to find out, but a part of me already knew that there was no future for the two of us.

So what happened now? Which voice did I listen to?

I climbed out of bed and pulled an oversized sweater over my head, and then made my way out to the living room only to find the couch empty. I wasn't sure whether I was relieved or not.

"Morning, baby girl," Mum called from the kitchen. "I made porridge if you want some."

"It's delicious," Brandon said.

I mashed my lips together. He was still here.

"Good morning, Taylor," he added.

"Hi," I replied. "Did Jesse come home?"

"Of course, honey, he's already left," Mum replied as she flicked her light brown fringe from her grey eyes. I looked a lot like my mother, only my eyes were more my father's shade, but a flat bronze rather than with golden hues.

"Left?" I asked. "Where?"

"To sign the lease and pick up the keys to your apartment. Remember, honey?"

I nodded slowly and slipped onto the stool beside Brandon. "Right."

"Have you packed up your stuff?" Brandon asked. "I can help you move in."

I rubbed my eyes. "Isn't your ute still somewhere on the side of the road?"

He smiled. "No, it's out the front. Jesse took me to replace the tyre earlier. It was completely split, like it had been slashed."

I stuck my finger in his porridge and tasted it. It was oat bran. I approved. Brandon pushed the bowl towards me.

"Wait, did you say *earlier*?" I asked. "What time is it exactly?"

"Eleven," Mum answered. "You slept in."

"Eleven?" I almost choked. "So, why the porridge?"

Mum shrugged. "I felt like a snack."

I scooped a spoonful into my mouth. "Of porridge?"

She nodded.

Brandon laughed at my expression.

"Sorry, were you eating this?" I asked.

He shook his head. "You can have it. It was my second bowl."

"Oh."

"So, honey, are you packed and ready to move into the new place?" Mum asked. "Jesse was hoping to start taking things today."

I ran the spoon around the rim of the bowl. There was some dry bran caked on the edge that I worked hard to chisel off. Brandon gave me a gentle nudge.

"Hm?" I said. "Sorry, Mum, did you say something?"

She sighed. "I asked if you'd had a chance to pack yet, Taylor."

"Oh, uh, no. But I don't really need to. I'm not taking any of my old stuff. All I need is my newer clothes, and I'll be fine."

"Just clothes? Are you planning on sleeping on the floor?" Brandon asked.

I glanced up at him. "You can't really pack a bed in a box, can you, smarty pants?"

"Touché."

Mum exhaled. "So, you're set then? And you're leaving… all the rest of your things here?"

"Yes, well, for now… if that's okay," I replied. "I was going to start packing them up and sending them to charity."

"Charity?" Mum and Brandon echoed.

I looked between them. "Yes, charity. Living out of a suitcase for a year taught me that I don't need a lot to get by. Someone less fortunate than me might appreciate them more than I ever could."

"That's very noble, honey, but as someone who bought you a lot of those things, I'd prefer it if you hung on to a few of them. You might change your mind, or want to pass them on to your own children."

I shrugged. "If you would like to keep them, then you're welcome to."

I heard her exhale, and then exit the kitchen. It was quiet except for the sound of Brandon's and my breathing, and the *clinking* of my spoon against the bowl as I ate.

"You're different," Brandon said. "A lot different to what I expected of you… from what I remember of you."

"I guess as much as I'd like to say you didn't know me very well before I left, I've done a lot of growing up since I was away," I answered. "So I guess you're off the hook."

He smiled, and his eyes penetrated mine. Not the same as the stranger's had—Harper, with the unforgettable green eyes—but in a way that made me feel like he cared. It warmed me.

"So, I really want to kiss you right now, but you said you needed time to think, so I just wanted you to know that," he whispered.

My heart responded in a sprint, causing the blood to rush to my cheeks. I didn't have an answer for him yet. I didn't know what I wanted, or whether I could trust myself with him. Being around him made me feel like the girl who was ignored all those years, it brought out all my insecurities. I still wasn't sure whether I could get past that feeling. I wanted to. I wished I could so I could get what I'd always wanted with Brandon, but I couldn't let myself go.

"Hey, sleepy," Jesse said, making me jump. My hands rested on my cheek to cover the blush. Brandon shuffled on his stool.

"Hey, Jesse," I answered. "How's the unit looking?"

"All ready to move in." He grinned. "B, we might need your ute to shift a few things."

Brandon nodded. "Sure."

"Do you know what you're bringing, Tay?" Jesse asked me. "Have you packed some things to take?"

I drew in a breath and blew it out. "Sort of, in a way, kind of."

"She's only bringing her new stuff," Brandon replied for me. "Something about getting used to living out of a suitcase."

Jesse's brow rose. "You're not bringing anything but clothes?"

"And her bed," Brandon added.

I shrugged. "Do I need anything else?"

Jesse frowned. "Guess not."

"Well, okay then." I smiled. "I'll make sure everything is ordered, and we can start the moving."

Jesse nodded. "Great."

I ate another spoonful of porridge and then pushed the bowl forward. I then spun on the stool towards my room. I took a step and then stopped and looked back at my brother.

"Hey, Jess?" I said.

His soft silver eyes glinted as his eyebrows lifted. "Yes, Tay?"

"This is going to be great, you know, us living together."

He nodded. "I know, Tay. I can't wait."

I pressed my lips into a smile and continued down to my childhood room. The time had come to pack up my life and decide which of it was worth bringing with me into the new chapter.

Phase Four
The Black Cat

Jesse and I were mostly moved into our new unit by nightfall. My new room was a bed surrounded by a mini-metropolis of boxes. I found that once I began sifting through my belongings, there was more that I wanted to keep than I remembered: mostly books, some trinkets, minimal photos, clothes and my uni things. It all seemed to pile up though; it was incredible how deceiving corners and drawers could be.

Sunday morning I was up relatively early compared to Saturday's sleep in. I had promised the vet that I would go and help out, so I spent the whole day assisting with clerical duties, and the odd veterinary aid. By the time I had finished, the sun was on its way to bed, and the Moon had stapled itself to the frosty clouds. The nights now were cold, and mostly clear, sending an eerie frosty haze over South Coast City.

I made my way to my car after work, feeling the fatigue from my mixed up sleeping patterns, and fumbled through my keys for the right one. They seemed oddly crowded now with my new house keys, and old house keys, coupled with my car keys. The mist that fell on the city seemed to weigh heavily on my head. I was not in the right mindset to think. Once I'd located the right key, I stuck it at the hole and missed entirely. It slipped through my fingers to the black concrete, under the rim of my car.

I reached down to retrieve them and felt a brush of fur on my hand. I frowned, and sunk to my knees, dropping my eye-line to peer underneath.

The small, raven coloured kitten *meowed* and licked my finger. It looked young, too young to be out of its litter and uncared for. It was shivering wildly, its hair sticking together in places. I cradled it in my hands and pulled it into my chest, picking up my keys as I rose to my feet to unlock my car.

It didn't move from my lap the whole drive home, but sat complacently, peering up at me with its mustard coloured eyes that seemed to glow in the blackness.

"Hey, Tay," Jesse said as I carefully propped the door open.

"Hey, Jess," I murmured. "Don't be mad."

He laughed and peered around the kitchen to where I stood at the door. "A cat?"

"It was under my car." I pouted. "It needs caring for."

"Lucky it was your car it was under then."

"So I can keep her?"

"Taylor, I'm not Mum and Dad." He laughed. "This is our place. You don't need to ask my permission."

I looked down at the kitten excitedly. "I'm going to name her Raven."

"Raven." Jesse nodded. "I like it."

*

I spent most of the evening taking care of my new pet, so when the Monday sun greeted me in the morning, I was ill-equipped to sit through classes for any length of time. Regardless, I hauled myself out of bed, put out some fresh water, chopped up some raw meat for Raven, and headed into uni. I'm not much of a coffee drinker, but by lunchtime, I had downed four and a half long blacks. My eyes were dark with bags, but as round as dinner plates. I looked like some kind of supernatural creature.

My head was buzzing, though everything was moving at half speed, so I decided stopping would be a bad move. I hadn't allowed myself to fully get over jetlag, so instead of taking a proper lunchbreak, I headed to the lab. I expected it to be empty, but when I opened the door, I found someone hovering over a microscope. His bronze hair stood out against the dark clothes he wore, and at my entrance, he didn't turn. It was almost as if he was expecting me.

"Hi," I sighed. "Sorry, I didn't think anyone would be here."

"You don't need to apologise, the lab is not mine to claim," he answered politely. "You are as welcome here as I am."

I closed the door behind me as he turned.

"Oh, Harper, it's you." I smiled. "Hello."

"Taylor." He nodded.

"What are you doing here? Are you a science major?"

He nodded. "So it seems."

"Obviously." I laughed nervously. "What are you studying?"

"Molecular biology," he replied.

"Wow."

He glanced up at me and smiled. His eyes were hypnotising, but they seemed familiar somehow. Almost like...

"Is everything okay?" he asked. That accent melted me like an icecap in the Sahara.

"I, um," I started. "This is going to sound crazy."

His brow furrowed, but his eyes didn't leave mine.

"It's just... your eyes, they're so peculiar. The colour, I mean," I said. He looked down shyly, and I tipped my head to get a better look. "I've only seen some that colour once before, but..."

He glanced up. "But?"

I shook my head. "Nothing, it's just... it was this beautiful, kind of tame, but wild wolf I encountered recently when I was driving home from the airport with my brother."

"Really."

I nodded and then looked down. "Crazy, huh?"

"Crazy," he agreed.

"Why is it so easy with you? I mean, I feel like I've known you forever."

He smiled and glanced back to his microscope. It reminded me of our last meeting in the darkness – when I had probably said too much and... hadn't he said that seeing him again would be a bad idea?

"I'm sorry, I'll leave you to work," I murmured. "I can come back another time."

He glanced up. "You don't have to go. As I said, you are as welcome here as I."

"I know, but I know how you prefer your own company."

He pressed his lips into a smile. "It's okay, you can stay."

"Unless…"

"Unless?"

"It's okay, I'll go," I said, turning towards the door.

"Taylor," he called. "Unless what?"

I drew in a breath. "I was just going to ask if you wanted to maybe grab a coffee or something. But I know that when we met, you said that you didn't want to see me…"

He nodded slowly. "Well, that wasn't very polite of me, was it?"

I shrugged.

"Actually, I recall saying that I would see you, but it was hard to explain," he answered.

I bit my lip. "What does that mean exactly?"

"It means I'd like to *grab* a coffee with you."

"Really?"

"Really." He nodded. "You seem surprised."

"I am."

He packed his books into a pile. "Shall we go?"

I followed him towards the door, and he pulled it open, stepping back to let me out first. I hesitated and then walked through. I wasn't used to chivalry.

"Do you like animals then?" he asked out of nowhere.

I looked at him curiously. "Yes. I'm actually studying to be a vet. How did you know that?"

He smiled. "You have the smell of cat on you."

"Oh," I sighed, suddenly feeling self-conscious. "Sorry, I rescued one last night. I didn't realise the smell was that bad."

"It's not," he answered.

I didn't quite believe him, but maybe because insecurity was my default setting.

"I'm sorry," he murmured. "I didn't mean to offend you. My sense of smell is just good. Honestly, you smell rather nice."

I smiled and felt myself blush.

We walked in comfortable silence to the coffee strip, bypassing all the brand-name, popular restaurants, until we reached a quiet side street. We made our way a quarter of the way down and stopped in front of a quaint, French-looking café named *Clair De Lune*.

"Is this okay?" he asked.

I couldn't seem to wipe the surprise from my face. I hadn't known this place existed, though admittedly, I hadn't wandered around here in over a year.

"Yes," I answered. "It's... just like the ones in Paris."

He smiled. "I know."

"You're French? Or at least you've spent time there."

He nodded. "My mother was French. I spent some time there, yes."

"You also lived in England," I said, not inflecting the question as a question.

"My father was English," he replied. "So yes, I was raised mainly in England."

"London?"

He shook his head. "Derbyshire. It's in the Midlands, next to Nottinghamshire."

"So when did you move to South Coast?" I asked.

Harper gestured for me to sit, and we found a table under the shelter of an olive tree which grew alongside the café.

"I used to visit here on vacations with my parents," he explained. "My godfather lives here. I officially moved here about a week and a half ago."

"Wow," I said. "You've only lived here for just over a week? What made you do that?"

He glanced down at the table. "Are you a coffee drinker, Taylor? Or do you prefer tea?"

I looked down as he nudged the menu towards me, completely forgetting that was the purpose of our outing. I peered at the words, and frowned, reaching into my bag for my reading glasses. As I cracked the box open, something small tumbled out. It was the tooth pendant I had found after he'd disappeared on the evening we'd first met.

"Oh," I sighed as his fingers reached out for it.

"Where did you find this?" he whispered.

"I found that in the park," I answered. "Is it yours?"

"Yes." He nodded, his voice becoming thick. "It belonged to my father."

"Belonged?"

"He died in a hunting accident."

"I'm sorry."

He nodded and curled the tooth in his hand. I glanced back down at my glasses and slipped them on, and the letters on the embossed card becoming clear to me. I ran my fingers through my hair as I read the selection of beverages. Each were in French with the English translation underneath.

"Have you eaten lunch?" Harper asked. "Or can I interest you in a *baguette* or *crêpe* or *pâtisserie*?"

I smiled and shook my head incredulously.

"What?" He smirked.

"You just... don't seem real that's all," I replied.

"What makes you think that I am?"

"Are you telling me you're a mythical character?"

His lips pulled into a twisted smile. "What if I am?"

"I'm even more intrigued," I answered.

His eyes glowed liquid emerald. The world seemed to disappear, and the noises around us fade away. We could have been in the middle of a warzone, but I wouldn't have noticed. What was it about Harper Lovett that drew me in? How did he make me forget about everything else that I thought was important to me?

"So, that guy you were with Friday," Harper said. "Is he going to be wondering where you are?"

I felt my brow furrow as I deciphered the meaning behind his words.

"Who? Brandon?" I asked. "We're not... I mean, he's not my boyfriend. He's just a friend of my brother's."

"I find it hard to believe that he's not interested in you."

I shook my head. "It's not that."

"You're not interested in him?"

"I don't know. I used to be, but I'm not sure now. I've changed a lot from the girl I used to be when I was infatuated with him. I don't know if he really likes me for me, or whether it's just because I look different."

He tipped his head. "What makes you think that?"

"He didn't see me before," I murmured. "I always felt invisible around him."

"And because of that you don't think he would like you for who you are?"

I shook my head. "No."

"That's silly," he sighed. "You didn't look bad before. Just because he overlooked you before shouldn't predetermine how he feels about you now."

"I know, but it does. Maybe I'm mistrusting of people's motives now; maybe I've just come to expect to be the punch line."

"Why are you so quick to believe all the bad things, but you won't believe the good?"

I smiled. "Because all the bad stuff is easier to believe."

"It's scary," he replied, glancing down. "Trusting people, and opening yourself up to them."

I nodded in agreement. "So what about you? Do you take your own advice?"

He glanced up, his eyes drawing me in again. "We were talking about you."

I laughed. "I guess that qualifies as a *no*."

He smiled politely. "So how long did you spend in Paris?"

"Just a weekend here and there," I answered; then frowned. "How did you know I spent time in Paris?"

"You said that this place looks just like the ones in Paris," he replied. "It's a long way to go from South Coast for only a weekend here and there."

I sighed. "Yes, it is from South Coast, but not from Italy. I spent a year working holiday there and only got back just before the start of the semester."

"Hence seeing the wolf on the way back from the airport *recently*."

"You do pay attention." I nodded impressively.

His eyes lowered to the menu. "Do you know what you'd like?"

"Well, I was thinking maybe…"

My eyes lifted as Harper reached out towards me as if he was about to cradle my face. My breathing was shallow as I anticipated the moment his skin would brush mine, but it didn't come. Instead, his hand touched my shoulder and withdrew, dropping something onto the table in front of us. I glanced at it and jumped at the menacing black spider between us.

"Black Widow Spider," he said. "The fourth most venomous spider in the world – noteworthy for the red markings on their body, but not to be confused with the redback."

My mouth was gaping open as it crawled across the table.

Harper smiled. "Nasty little things."

"That… that was on me?" I breathed; then shivered. "Oh my gosh. I could have died."

He caught the spider between his napkin before it reached the edge of the table, and rose to his feet.

"I wouldn't have let you die," he replied. "They have good anti-venom available now."

I sat back deep in thought as Harper paced away to set it free in the shrubbery opposite. What was going on?

When he returned, he was smiling infinitesimally.

"Are you all right, Taylor?" he asked.

I sighed. "I don't want to sound paranoid, but I think the world has it in for me."

I expected him to laugh, but instead, he frowned. "Why?"

"Ever since I got back, weird things have been happening," I replied, shaking my head. "I couldn't tell you how many people in the past week have asked if I have a death wish."

Harper looked troubled by the idea, almost as if he was actually taking my complaint seriously. I examined his face, taking the opportunity without the distraction of his eyes to memorise the shape of his jaw, the chiselling of his cheekbones, the clearly defined contour of his lips, and the pucker which appeared between his brows when he seemed lost in thought. He was beautiful, and I felt terrible for the fact that a large part of my attraction to him was based on looks, but it didn't make it less true. But there was more to it than that. There was the way he listened to me, the way he opened doors for me, and the way he made me feel protected from whatever might come my way. He made me feel like there was more to the world than what I knew of it, and I couldn't explain why.

"Taylor?" someone said, but not in Harper's accent.

I looked up. "Brandon."

He glanced over at Harper with an air of misplaced superiority, and then looked back to me. "What are you doing?"

"Having lunch," I replied, as April appeared at his side.

"Don't you have class?"

"Don't you?"

He smiled and held his hand towards Harper. "Hi, I'm Brandon."

Harper just looked at him. "I know who you are."

Brandon's hand fell away. "And you are?"

Harper glanced at me with a look of discomfort, and I could see that he didn't like the introduction of new people, especially new people who were questioning him. He preferred his own company, and it was against his norm to even be in my company given our lack of familiarity.

"This is Harper," I answered for him. "We're studying science together."

Brandon nodded as if he had the right to give approval on who I spent time with. April smiled widely.

"I bet you're really good at chemistry," she said with a lift of her eyebrow.

"I'm not a chemistry major," Harper replied indifferently, and I couldn't help but laugh at April's confused expression.

"Clearly," Brandon mumbled below his breath. Harper glanced at him evenly.

"It was a pleasure to be in your company, Taylor, but I should go," Harper said looking back to me.

I felt panic flood. "No, Harper, please stay. We haven't even ordered yet."

"Apologies," he answered as he rose to his feet. "Another time, perhaps."

"Promise?"

He smiled weakly. "Goodbye, Taylor."

Harper's eyes locked on mine, drawing me in like a lasso before releasing me with a kind of whiplash. He gave Brandon a departing glare, and fleeting glance at April, before turning away and disappearing into the street. His final words churned around in my head as April sat down, and Brandon pulled up a chair. A sinking feeling inside me felt like Harper's goodbye was more final than I wanted it to be.

*

For the next few days, I just couldn't get him out of my head. Those hypnotic iced green eyes that were so unique and strange, but somehow so familiar. I tried to stop myself from thinking about him, from dwelling on the unattainable, but my mind kept returning to the forbidden territory. I was enthralled, captivated, and felt like the same sense of insecurity my former self knew well. It frightened me feeling this way again like I had lost control of my life, but I couldn't describe the bond I felt with him. The instant connection didn't make sense to me, and I felt as though if I didn't pursue it, I would be betraying myself. I tried to find him again, but it was as though he had vanished just like that first night he disappeared with only the tooth pendant as a trace that he actually existed. This time I had nothing but the memory, and if I was honest, I was starting to doubt even that.

"So, you and Brandon have been spending a bit of time together," Jesse said on Thursday afternoon as he flopped beside me on the couch. "Should I be worried?"

I stroked Raven's fur, and she purred against my hand. "About Brandon? No."

He looked over at me. "What's going on, Taylor?"

"Nothing," I answered, feeling my forehead crease. "Why?"

"You seem distracted," he replied, reaching to pat Raven's head; she leant into his touch.

"I guess I have a lot of my mind."

"Anything I can help with?"

I shook my head. "Mostly just adjusting to being back home."

"Mostly? Do you think you're taking on too much, working at the vet while trying to settle back into study?"

"No." I frowned. "Why? Do you?"

"Maybe."

"Jess, do you think that people can change?"

He shrugged. "Depends on the person."

I nodded.

"Why? Who's changing?" he asked.

"I just," I started slowly. "I don't know… Brandon maybe. But then there's Harper—"

"Who?"

"Harper. The guy… oh… I met this guy at the back to uni party. He's a science major, and we went out for coffee on Monday, well, almost, but then Brandon showed up, and he left."

Jesse blinked. "Right."

"And now I can't stop thinking about him," I murmured.

"Who?" Jesse asked. "Brandon or this Harper guy?"

I glanced at my brother. "Harper, and sort of Brandon, I don't know."

Jesse inhaled and let it out slowly. He'd never had to deal with anything like this with me before.

"So, when you talk about people changing, you're really asking whether Brandon has changed since you've been gone," he clarified.

I nodded. "But then I think maybe it's just me who's changed; and can I really hold against him that he notices me now because of how I look when I only liked him before because I thought he was attractive? Doesn't that make me a hypocrite?"

"Taylor, I think you're over thinking things a bit." He chuckled. "Do you like him now for who he is?"

I exhaled. "He is certainly charming."

"Yes. It sounds like there is a 'but' though."

"But is that enough?" I asked. "When I'm with Harper, the world seems to stop… or rather, I want it to."

Jesse tipped his head. "Well, I think you have your answer… so what's the problem then?"

I shrugged. "I haven't seen him since Monday, it's like he's just disappeared."

"That's only a few days, Tay. He might not have had classes since then," Jesse answered. "You don't need to rush things, just relax, and everything will turn out how it's meant to."

I bit my lip. Jesse was right of course, but I couldn't help but feel an element of urgency in finding Harper again. It wasn't rational, but it was there. I felt like one way or another, I was running out of time.

"Is there something else bothering you?" he asked, tipping my lowered chin up towards him. "You're not worried about the housewarming tomorrow night are you?"

I groaned. "Right, the party."

"April is coming, isn't she?" Jesse smiled. "Should be fun."

"Mm." I nodded.

April was the only one of my friends coming. I didn't really keep in touch with anyone while I was away. Jesse was the closest thing I had to a best friend these days.

"Well, if you see your friend Harper again, you should invite him," Jesse said, and my heart squeezed at the thought of him. "That might make things more interesting for you."

I felt my cheeks heat up, and focused more intently on Raven, hoping Jesse didn't notice the change. If he did, he didn't say anything. Jesse always knew precisely what to say and when to say it.

*

I was supposed to work for the vet after uni on Friday, but my shift was cancelled. So instead, I headed to the library to put off going home for as long as I could. Jesse was going to try and leave work a bit earlier to set up, and Brandon, being the chief organiser, was going to head over mid-afternoon to do most of the legwork. I wasn't avoiding him, well not officially, but I wasn't ready to face him alone because I knew it would just confuse me more. Ideally, I wanted to see Harper first to see if there was even the remotest of possibilities that he'd ever want to hang out again.

"Taylor," whispered a silky accent.

I jumped and turned quickly, nearly falling off my chair. "Harper."

He smiled weakly. "Hello."

"I've been looking for you," I said without thinking. My eyes closed in realisation. "I mean, hi."

"Why have you been looking for me?"

I shrugged. "I was beginning to think I just dreamed you up."

"I'm hardly a dream," he answered.

I couldn't agree with him, so I instead changed the subject. "I'm sorry about Monday."

"What is there to be sorry about?" he asked.

"I'm sorry you left."

"It wasn't you."

I blinked. It wasn't the answer I wanted, but it was the best I was going to get. He looked over my face for a moment, his expression conflicted as if he was debating whether to stay or go. My heart hammered urgently as I racked my brain for something to say to make him stay.

"I'm having a party tonight," I blurted out, as he took half a step backwards. He stopped and rolled forward.

"A party?" he asked.

"Well, it's more a gathering. My brother and I just moved into our own place, and we are having a few people around to mark the occasion. Kind of like a housewarming. You're very welcome to come."

He looked down, and I could almost guess his reply before he verbalised it. "I'm not sure if that's a good idea."

"Why not?"

His eyes found mine. "I just…"

"I get it. You don't like crowds."

"I'm sorry."

I shook my head. "I just thought it would be nice to hang out. I'm not really looking forward to this thing anyway. I thought that you being there might make it more bearable."

He chuckled, and the sound caught me off guard. I glanced up to look at him curiously.

"You hardly know me." He smiled. "Yet you give me so much more credit than I deserve."

"Maybe."

"What is the address?"

My eyebrows lifted in hope. "You're going to come?"

"I won't make any promises, but I will see what I can do," he said.

It was good enough for me. I turned back to my notebook, scribbled my address, and then handed it to him with shaky hands.

*

"You're home." Brandon smiled as I stepped inside the apartment. Jesse and I had only been living there a few days, but it was already beginning to feel like home.

"You're here," I murmured, pulling my keys out the front door.

He raised his eyebrows. "You off to save animals?"

"No, they don't need me today."

"Well I need you," he replied.

I stopped and looked up at him properly for the first time. He was nearly dressed in jeans and a T-shirt with some kind of designer label on it that I didn't bother myself to register. He was sitting on our couch, or more lounging, with one of my veterinary science books on his lap.

I folded my arms. "What are you doing Brandon?"

"Reading."

"Aren't you supposed to be setting up?"

"It's done." He shrugged. "I brought the food over; the drinks are in the bath waiting for ice, and you and Jesse keep the place spotless since you're hardly ever home."

I pressed my lips together as Raven jumped up onto the seat beside him, and curled herself against his side. He didn't look up from the book but reached out to stroke her. I could hear her purring from where I still stood inside the door.

"Brandon," I sighed. "Why are you reading my textbook?"

"It was this or the surgical book that Jesse uses to level out the desk, but that was wedged pretty good under the leg," he replied.

I couldn't help but laugh. "So what have you learnt?"

"Cows have four stomachs," he answered.

"That's not in the book."

He laughed and closed it. "I know."

"So, when is this thing starting?"

"When Jesse gets home, I'm breaking out the beer," he said.

"Then you should probably get ice," I replied, glancing at my watch. It was almost five thirty. "He'll be home anytime now."

"Mm. Good plan. You want to come with?"

"No, I think I'll just get a shower."

His eyes lingered down my body and then dropped back to the book. "Okay, I'd better get going if I want the beer chilled for Jesse."

"Right," I sighed and started for my room.

"Hey, Taylor," he called.

I glanced over my shoulder at him.

"Save me a dance later," he said with a smile.

I rolled my eyes and continued to my room. I wasn't sure how I was going to get through the next few hours, but I wasn't much looking forward to it. Despite the fact I may look the part now, I wasn't sure I fit into Brandon's world of fake smiles and twirling.

The night went as expected and felt much like the Friday before. I played hostess as much as I could for Jesse's benefit, while April swooned over his friends, including Brandon, who didn't seem to mind at all. Brandon spent a decent amount of time flirting with April, and a couple of the other girls there, while temporarily turning his attention back to me at regular intervals. I couldn't deny that I liked the attention, but it did bother me that his affection seemed divided between us. It also bothered me that, amidst her flirting, April dared to whisper to me: *"Don't fall in love with Brandon, Taylor, he's not the type of guy you fall in love with because he'll just break your heart."*

It was then that I decided to make a break for it. So, while they both were busy with their antics, I headed out the front for some quiet under the black velvet comfort of the stars. Raven found me, brushing her head against my ankle, and I picked her up, stroking her midnight fur as I took in the stillness of the evening.

"Not having fun?" the accented voice said from the darkness. I came to find comfort in the echoed voice from the abyss.

"No, not particularly," I replied.

Harper stepped into the light as Raven hissed at him, the hackles of her hair standing up around her neck and up her back. I jumped as she threw a paw in his direction to scratch him, but instead sank them into the skin of my forearm. I yelped and dropped her.

"Ouch," I gasped. "What is wrong with you?"

Raven hissed again in Harper's direction and darted off into the night. I might have otherwise cared about her tantrum if my arm wasn't budding with thick red droplets of blood. Harper stepped forward and pulled a piece of fabric from his pocket, wrapping it around my wound. His hands were warm despite the coolness of the night.

"I'm sorry about my cat," I said. "I don't know what's wrong with her. She's usually really good with people."

He smiled. "Cats have never really liked me."

"So, you came."

"Yes. I wasn't sure if I was going to."

"Me neither," I answered honestly. "But I'm glad you did."

"Why?"

I shrugged. "I don't know. I feel safer with you around."

He frowned. "If you don't feel safe, then why are you outside?"

"I'm more afraid of the darkness inside." I laughed. "And I was looking for the Moon."

"There is no Moon tonight," he replied.

"So I see." I nodded.

His eyes flickered to mine, then back to my arm. The bleeding was drying now, and slowly beginning to stop. His fingers brushed the crease of my elbow over four welts.

"You were stung?" he asked.

"Wednesday," I answered. "Somehow a small swarm of bees got into my car, and I couldn't get them out the window in time. Lucky I'm not allergic."

He frowned. "Lucky."

"I never used to be so much of a magnet for misfortune," I said, peeling back the handkerchief to reveal the four scratches in my forearm. "Oh well, at least they match the ones on my shoulder."

Harper's frown deepened. "On your shoulder?"

"Yes," I answered, turning back my top to reveal the healing scar. "Something scratched me the night I saw that wolf. Some woman wearing white, I think. I mean, I didn't really see her, but I heard her scream."

Harper swallowed. "Scream."

I nodded. "It was horribly loud. I thought my eardrums would burst."

"Oh, Taylor," he breathed.

Any other time the whisper of my name might have whipped my heart into a sprint, but there was an edge to his tone that made my blood run cold, a kind of terror running through me, icing my veins. There was a solemn and aged wisdom in his expression that frightened me, almost as if he knew something more than he said, or what he wanted to say.

"Taylor?" Brandon called. "Are you… where are you?"

I looked in his direction and stepped forward, pushing Harper back into the shadows. He clutched at my arm as I fell against him, nearly tripping over my own feet.

"Taylor?" my name echoed.

Harper's brow creased, and I raised my finger to my lips. His eyebrows rose in the darkness, and it was as if he could see me just as perfectly as if it was daylight.

He lifted his finger and then nodded. "He's gone."

"Sorry," I said. "I just can't deal with him right now."

"What's to deal?" he asked.

"The last time he interrupted us, you left."

"Taylor, I don't think…" he sighed, and then looked down at my arm and seemed to reconsider what he was going to say. "I need to go."

"What?" I frowned. "Why?"

He shook his head. "It's not… I mean, I will see you again soon. Are you free for coffee tomorrow?"

I nodded mutely, not remembering whether I needed to work, but vowing to call in sick if I did.

"I'll meet you at *Clair De Lune* at one," he replied. "So, try to keep yourself from harm's way until then."

"Deal," I answered; and he disappeared into the night.

I stood motionless, not sure whether moving would shatter the memory. He wanted to see me again. He wanted to see me tomorrow. What had changed? Why had he said my name with such pity when he learned of my scratches?

"Taylor, there you are," Brandon's voice said. "I've been looking for you."

95

I was still frozen but managed to tear myself from my thoughts long enough to glance over at him. I stared at him for a long moment before realisation hit.

"Taylor," he repeated. It startled me, his voice, not the volume or the tone, but the pronunciation of the pronoun. It was not quite sober.

"Brandon," I said, turning my body towards him.

"Taylor," he garbled again, stumbling into the light to reveal himself.

I frowned at him as he smiled dumbly. There was no denying that he was intoxicated.

"You're drunk," I sighed.

"N-n-no I'm n-not," he slurred, and then laughed at himself as if he'd just told a humorous joke. "Okay, maybe a little."

"Get away from me."

"No, not until you s'plain to me what you were doing with that… that guy the other day," he replied, reaching a hand to grip my shoulder. I pushed it off.

"I don't need to explain anything to you," I answered. "Leave me alone."

"He's wrong for you, Taylor; you shouldn't be with him."

"I didn't ask your opinion, and I'm not talking to you when you're like this."

"Like what?"

"Drunk, Brandon," I said.

He closed his eyes and stumbled a little. "I'm not drunk."

I shook my head. "You haven't changed a bit."

He blinked through unseeing eyes as my words slowly sunk in.

"You know what?" he replied. "I'm sick of feeling not good enough for you. I don't have to prove anything to you. This is me, this is who I am, and if you don't like it, then you can just..."

"Brandon," I sighed.

"No!" he shouted. "Just get off your high horse, Taylor. We all know you were hard-done-by when you were fat and invisible, but get over yourself 'cause I'm not changing who I am... and to be honest, I don't know if there is anyone else I haven't pretended to be just so you would accept me."

I recoiled as if he'd slapped me and, in a way, he had. Everything he'd said was precisely what I had felt before, and I was putting him through everything I had experienced without being a physical outcast.

"I... I'm... I didn't mean to make you feel that way," I said.

"Whatever," he mumbled, ruffling his sandy blond hair. "You used to be nice."

"No," I answered. "I used to be ignored."

His forehead creased as he appraised what I was saying, and then he slowly turned and stumbled back the way he'd come. I could hear his sporadic footsteps graze the concrete as he walked up towards the house. After a few measured seconds, the step-falls gradually disappeared.

I wasn't sure what had just happened—whether I'd missed something, and Brandon had broken up with me despite the fact we were never dating—but I knew that I had caused it.

I leant back against my car and thought over what he'd said, and it made my heart sink to realise that he was absolutely right. I was a hypocrite. I had been since I'd gotten back. I had been acting like I was entitled to be treated better, just because I looked better. And maybe I did, but that did not mean I deserved any special treatment. Maybe Brandon had changed, maybe he hadn't. That wasn't really the issue here. The issue was that I had changed, and it wasn't for the better.

The thought broke me down. The mere concept that I had become someone who used to torment me, and I didn't even realise it until the person who had tormented me called me on it. I couldn't face anyone, I didn't want to. I wasn't in the mood for a party, and I wished that everyone would just leave so I could wallow in my self-pity.

I stayed outside in the dark for hours, maybe longer, until the voices inside quietened down, and the music faded to a dull thrumming. It was well after midnight, it had to be. Some people had left, while others had apparently decided to stay the night.

I made sure everyone was gone before sneaking back in, and I was both disappointed and thankful to find a trail of leftover food still lying around the deserted house. I gathered what I could, aware that my willpower and discipline were severely compromised by my emotional state. I didn't care that it was wrong, and I didn't care that I had gone through hell to lose the weight. All I knew was I needed food—the sugary, carb-loaded, fatty kind—and I couldn't stop myself once I'd started.

I retreated to my room and was a woman possessed. I didn't just fall off the wagon. I threw myself off. And I could feel the effects already start to dominate in my body. It felt wrong.

I couldn't fathom it, but it was a strange feeling, like a feeling of no control – of the extreme loss of control. I no longer had command over my body, because the urge to eat was overpowering. Beyond mind power, it was a drive. I couldn't stop myself. I could barely see anything except the food. I couldn't smell anything except the scent of sugar that hung in the air, drawing me towards it. I blanked into autopilot and was powerless. My mouth watered as my muscles responded to the impulse, and as the sweet nectar touched my lips, I was no longer myself. I was her, that other girl, the destructive girl who was severely helpless and depressed. I was weak, and I had succumbed to the monster inside me that had taken my life away from me once before. I was losing it again; only this time I had more to lose.

After the fourth helping, despite the fact I couldn't stop myself, I felt ill. My body was rejecting the foreign introduction, and my heart thumped rapidly in response to the sudden sugary intake. If food was a drug, I would have overdosed. Flatlined.

By the time I'd mustered control of the compulsion to keep eating, I wanted to throw up. I dragged myself into the bathroom and tried, but the impulse was unfamiliar to me. I'd never been strong enough, or weak enough, to purge my food.

I gave up with watering eyes and curled up on the bathroom floor, crying myself to a restless stupor that would bring me to the morning that I didn't really want to face.

Phase Five
The Eyes in the Shadows

"Taylor," Jesse whispered as he shook my shoulder to wake me.

My body hurt, and there was a sickly sweet taste in my mouth. My eyelashes were still stuck together with teardrops that hadn't dried. I fleetingly wondered what I looked like, and then decided I didn't care.

"Jesse," I answered flatly.

"What happened?" he sighed, sitting beside me. He placed a glass of water on the tiles and brushed my hair back from my face.

"I don't know why I bothered... I feel terrible... I'm a bad person," I croaked as I tried to sit. My stomach lurched, and I resented the fact that I couldn't make myself sick.

"Why?"

"Last night, Brandon said—"

"I hope this isn't about something Brandon said," Jesse sighed. "Taylor, he was wasted last night, so I wouldn't take anything that came out of his mouth too seriously."

I exhaled. "He was right. I've turned into someone I used to hate."

"So change." He shrugged. "Change back."

"I can't… or don't want to. I was miserable before."

He tipped up my chin. "You're miserable now."

It felt like my frown was etched into my face. "I ate a lot last night. A lot of bad food."

"It's okay," he whispered. "It was a slip-up."

I closed my eyes. "I'm scared."

"You'll be fine Taylor."

"I don't want to put on all the weight again," I murmured. "I think I've already put on weight since being back."

"Taylor, it takes more than one meal to put on twenty-two kilos," he said rationally. "Now why don't you get a shower, and I'll make us scrambled eggs for breakfast?"

I nodded and pulled myself up. "Is Brandon still here?"

"I'll make sure he's gone by the time you get out."

"Thanks," I sighed. It was cowardly and unreasonable, but I wasn't in a sound state of mind.

"Feeling better?" Jesse asked as I forced the last bit of egg into my mouth. I didn't feel like eating ever again because I could still feel the sugar sitting in my chest, but I made myself eat it. I'd read enough about dieting to know that skipping meals was not the answer.

"No," I replied.

Jesse sat down opposite me and folded his arms. "What am I going to do with you?"

"Shoot me," I murmured, and then laughed flatly.

Jesse didn't even break a smile. "I'm worried about you."

"Don't be. I'll get back on track. It just might take me a bit."

"Not just because of the food stuff," he replied. "It's more than that. You're more than that."

I pressed my lips together. "I might go for a run."

"It's raining and windy out there," Jesse sighed. "Just give it a day."

I breathed a laugh. "Right, I'll be fine. I'll see you when I get back."

I hadn't believed my brother about the rain or wind, but outside it was like a cyclone. I didn't care. I ran anyway, braving the gale force winds, and ice cold rain that hit me like needles and blinded my path. I ran until I wanted to vomit and then ran some more. I tried to run away the hatred I felt for myself, but it clung to me like stubborn cellulite. I slowed my steps, and rubbed the rain from my eyes, stopping underneath an olive tree and let the tears of frustration and exertion mix with the tears from the sky.

Something was wrong. Very wrong.

Nothing added up any more.

What was happening to me? Who was this person, this different, other, person that seems so familiar, but so foreign at the same time?

I'd always seen things in black and white because it was... it was simple, wasn't it?

But it didn't fit.

It wasn't right.

It didn't add up.

As the sun tried to shine through the raincloud, I frowned at the sky, wondering when life seemed to get complicated.

103

When it stopped being summer or winter and became a mixture of the two. Transitional seasons, that's what people called them. Seasons where it wasn't hot or cold, it was a combination of the two: both seasons in one day, or a mash-up where you seemed to feel warm and chilled at the same time. I didn't trust it. It wasn't something real, something tangible. Grey.

Why did things need to be so hard? Why couldn't I just be happy, and accept myself like other people seemed to?

I could feel my blood speed up in my thumping veins; feel every pulse as it tried to push the thickened liquid through my vessels.

Yes, I thought losing the weight would make me better, different, or at least something, but instead it made me shallow, vain, and condemning. I hadn't always been this way, I couldn't have been. When I first trimmed down, hadn't I been happy? Hadn't I found Leo? Hadn't Leo liked me?

I didn't even know who I was any more, because I was so far from any person I recognised. In Italy, I had at least been me, the old me with the new look. Here, being back in South Coast, I had morphed into this other person—this new person to match the new look—and I didn't like her very much.

I hung my head and watched as the raindrops trickled from the ends of my hair. I had lost my elastic a few kilometres back, and my hair was now tangled and unmanageable. It was like the cherry on top of the last twenty-four hours.

It came out of nowhere, or at least I didn't see it until it was colliding with my temple. The branch of the tree above me bounced to the floor, and I gripped my head as the red liquid streamed down my palm and forearm, dripping off my elbow to the ground.

I stumbled, sucking air through my teeth and made for the open. The raindrops burnt with cold as they continued to strike my skin.

My head hurt, it felt wrong.

My heart protested at the pressure it was under.

My head.

I clutched at my temples, feeling the beads of cold, clammy sweat form like droplets of water being forced through a pillowcase. My head felt like it was going to explode.

My hands began to shake violently in response to the chemical reaction that was churning in my body and the trauma to my head.

I was going to pass out, that was a sure thing. I was going to die… perhaps… it sure felt like it anyway.

As I felt my heart stutter and the pressure in my head peak, I made the promise to myself: if I survived this, something would need to change.

My legs buckled beneath me as the pressure got too much, gravity tackling me to the ground with a hefty thump. As my eyes rolled back in my head, and I felt the warmth of blood ooze from my ear, I thought I saw a pair of yellow eyes glaring at me from the shadows.

My eyes stooped closed.

Something was wrong.

*

I had a dream while I was unconscious. At least I think I was unconscious, and I think it was a dream. I dreamt of the wolf I'd encountered that night coming back from the airport. I imagined that I ran my fingers through its sepia coloured fur, and stroked its thick mane. I dreamt of its intelligent, hypnotic eyes peering up at me. The wolf blinked, and suddenly it was Harper staring back at me. He smiled and closed his eyes, and everything faded to black, and then there were other eyes; haunting, yellow eyes looking out at me through the blackness. They scared me, these eyes. They were cold and menacing.

I inhaled and opened my eyes, hearing a beeping beside me and jumped.

"Shh," a hushed voice said. "You're in the hospital."

I looked around and noticed his hair first, the blond scruffiness of the boy that my heart used to trip over all the time. His hand enclosed over mine, but I didn't feel comforted, I felt betrayed.

"Hey." He smiled and kissed my hand lightly. "Welcome back."

I pulled it away. I couldn't handle it. I couldn't handle him being here. Not with the way he felt about me, it was as if the universe was taunting me.

"Brandon? What are you doing here?" I asked, and my voice sounded rough.

Brandon's light blue eyes glanced to the side. "You scared us all for a while there. You lost some blood from that knock on your head."

I frowned. "That doesn't explain why…"

"I don't want to make a big thing of it," he whispered, resting his hand on the bandage in the crease of his elbow.

"What happened to you? Did you get hurt too?"

"Like I said, you'd lost some blood."

"You donated blood?" I asked. "To who?"

"You, dummy, who else?"

"But… you're not my blood type. Where's Jesse?"

"He's got low iron or something, so pathology wouldn't let him donate," he replied, tipping his head. "How do you know what blood type I am?"

"You said once that you were something else, and I remember it wasn't what I am." I half shrugged. I hurt all over.

"I'm a universal donor." He smirked. "My blood is literally worth bottling."

"Oh."

"Mm." He smiled. "I've got to say though, I am feeling a little woozy. It's going to take a while for you to pay me back for this."

"I didn't ask you to donate," I sighed.

"I know. So, I don't even get a thank you?"

"Thank you."

He leant forward and took my hand again. I tried to pull it away, but I was too weak.

"I'm sorry for what I said last night," he whispered. "Jesse said you were upset this morning. I didn't mean to upset you."

"Didn't you?"

"Not really. I guess I'm just not used to not getting what I want."

"And what is that?" I asked; though a part of me knew.

"You," he sighed. "As if you didn't know."

"I just don't know why."

Brandon shook his head incredulously. "Why do you need to question it?"

"I'm a science major, we question everything."

He laughed and leant in, entrapping me with his lips. I heard my heart respond to the embrace on the monitor, and felt my cheeks burn.

"Hey, you're awake," Jesse's voice said.

Brandon sat back and smiled smugly, and I looked towards my brother.

"Hey, Jesse," I breathed.

"You," he growled. "You scared the hell out of me."

"I'm sorry," I answered. "Really."

Jesse shook his head as another figure appeared beside him, and my heart gave another squeeze, whipping into a sprint. I saw Brandon's gaze trace to the monitor before following mine to the doorway, and then his face hardened.

"Harper." I smiled. "You're here."

He smiled back. "Didn't I tell you to stay out of harm's way until I saw you again?"

I chuckled; it hurt. "Yes, I think you did. Sorry."

"Harper?" Jesse asked, turning towards him. "Taylor has mentioned you. I'm Jesse, her brother."

"Pleasure." Harper nodded, accepting Jesse's hand. "She has mentioned you also."

"What are you doing here?" Brandon asked curtly.

Harper looked down at him unapologetically. "I'm the one who found her."

"You were?" I asked.

Harper glanced at me. "When you didn't show at the café, I went looking for you."

"Lucky you did," Jesse said. "Taylor had lost a lot of blood after suffering head trauma, and began to show signs of hypothermia."

"Thanks, Doctor Mistry," I sighed. "Do you guys mind if I talk to Harper alone for a moment?"

"Why?" Brandon frowned.

"Sure," Jesse answered, rolling his eyes. He patted Brandon on the shoulder, and Brandon reluctantly stood and followed him out. I exhaled impatiently as he glared at Harper as he passed him.

Harper waited until they were gone and then walked over, taking vigil by my bedside. His eyes were like a pouting puppy dog's, and twinkled as if we were having a wordless conversation, wordless, but somehow deep. I allowed myself to get lost in them, deciphering the shades of olive and flecks of emerald that coloured them.

We were both silent for a long time, and then he looked down, and words were necessary.

109

"Thank you," I whispered. "For looking out for me. I feel like you're always saving me."

He glanced up, but instead of smiling, he frowned. "I wish you didn't always need saving."

"Sorry."

He hung his head and leant toward me. "These things that are happening to you… you need to be careful, Taylor."

I breathed a laugh. "I'm trying."

"Try harder," he answered earnestly. His eyes were urgent and ancient in their concern.

My forehead creased as I read the desperation in his expression. "Is there something going on that you're not telling me? Do you know something?"

"Honey?" another voice said as my mother appeared in the doorway. "There you are. Are you okay?"

"Mum," I said. Her timing could not have been worse.

She shook her head, and hastened towards me, not noticing as Harper rose from the chair and slipped out the door. The monitor beeps quickened as he left, but it was no good. I may as well have been strapped to the bed.

The doctors kept me in overnight for observation, but I was discharged on Sunday around midday. Jesse took me home and made up a bed for me on the couch since I'd refused to go back to bed. I didn't bother arguing with him, so took the opportunity to catch up on some uni work. My head was still a little tender, but at least it still worked.

Aside from the sore head, which now had nine stitches where the branch had hit it above my right ear, my ego was also badly bruised. Unfortunately, I was pretty sure that wouldn't heal as quickly as the broken skin.

"Can I get you anything else?" Brandon asked. "I could make you some tea?"

"No," I replied, focusing extra hard on my textbook. "Thanks."

Brandon had arrived about an hour after Jesse, and I had gotten back from the hospital. He had been extra helpful in tending to my every need, but I wasn't sure how to take it. I didn't know if I'd missed something somewhere, but it seemed an awful lot like something you'd expect of a boyfriend.

"Okay, just let me know." He smiled, reaching out to brush my cheek. I leant away from it and bit my lip.

"Hey, Brandon," I said. "Um, what's going on?"

He tipped his head. "What do you mean?"

"I mean, why are you here?"

"I thought you might want some help settling back in."

I nodded slowly. "But, Jesse can do that."

He breathed a laugh, glancing at my brother who was suddenly very busy in the kitchen.

"Well then, I just thought you might like to, you know, hang out," he answered.

"I see."

"Is this about that Harper guy?" he asked.

I frowned. "What?"

"I mean, you've been seeing him a lot lately—"

"I've seen him twice in the past week, not that it's any of your business."

111

"It's not?" he asked. "Okay."

I opened my mouth, trying to phrase the words I never thought I'd say. "Brandon, we're not together, you and I. You get that, right?"

He recoiled as if I'd thrown a bucket of water on him.

"I mean, I appreciate what you're doing, and I don't mind hanging out with you, but we're not dating or anything," I continued when he didn't speak. "I don't think I should be with anyone right now; I'm still trying to kind of, find my feet again."

He seemed speechless, and I felt intense guilt seep through me.

"Right." He huffed. "Well, I should go."

I inhaled to stop him, but couldn't get the words out. Jesse peered over at me with saucer-round eyes and a mouth that was half open in surprise.

The front door closed, and I shook my head. "Was I too harsh?"

Jesse's mouth closed. "I don't quite know what just happened then."

"Did I miss something when I got hit in the head?" I asked. "Were we dating?"

Jesse laughed incredulously. "I... you... he..."

"When did everything get so complicated?"

Jesse smiled, and Raven jumped up beside me on the couch, curling up on my stomach. She peered up at me with big glowing eyes and rested her head on my chest. As I stared into her golden eyes, I couldn't help but think about that other pair

112

of eyes that watched me, the ones I had caught sight of before I'd blacked out. Had I imagined them, or were they real? Was something, or someone, watching me? And if so, what? Or scarier still, who?

*

"Taylor, can I talk to you?" Brandon murmured on Monday morning. I was struggling a bit with the strap of my bag, and the way I walked made my head pulse uncomfortably. Jesse had insisted I stay home, but I told him I'd just leave after he did, so as a compromise, he'd dropped me in and would pick me up afterwards. I'd won that battle but lost the war when it came to working at the vet. I called it a compromise for today, at least.

"Not now, Brandon. I'm running late for class," I sighed.

"Please, it'll only take a second."

"I don't have a second," I answered. I wasn't prepared for any kind of confrontation, especially on a Monday morning.

"Taylor, would you wait?" Brandon called.

"I don't have time," I said. "I'll just catch you later."

"You're always walking away from me," he yelled. "What's that about?"

I exhaled. "Take it as a hint."

"Taylor, just stop," he exclaimed, reaching out to grab my wrist. I felt myself being pulled back, and pivoted, landing up against the wall of the building with Brandon's eyes boring into mine. My head bounced lightly off the wall. It sent a throbbing pain through it, making me groan.

"Right, now that I have your attention," he said.

"Let her go," a silky voice thundered. I glanced over and was somewhat relieved to see Harper. That relief quickly replaced with excitement. However, this emotion was not reflected on Brandon's face, and the anger was almost tangible as he turned slowly towards him.

"Excuse me?" Brandon asked slowly. "Are you talking to me?"

"Yes." Harper nodded. "Kindly remove your hold on Taylor, or I will do it for you."

My mouth, which had been slightly ajar with wonder, snapped shut as I glanced back to Brandon who was now turning a shade of purple. It worked though, and slowly he stepped away from me, squaring his shoulders at Harper.

Now that I was free of Brandon's muscular cage, I was a little anxious that Harper might pay the price for it. Though to Harper's advantage, the street was filling up with spectators, and even Brandon wouldn't risk causing a scene that could result in the dampening of his reputation. Whatever that was.

"Taylor, are you all right?" Harper asked, his piercing green eyes fixed on Brandon's like a predator might observe its prey.

"Y-yes," I replied, gripping my head as it spun.

"Who the hell are you anyway?" Brandon spat. "You don't even know her."

114

Harper's eyes narrowed, casting a dark shadow over his light green eyes. Everything seemed to be moving in slow motion, and I could barely comprehend that these two highly eligible men were in some form fighting over me. Regardless, my head seemed to pound with the slight knock, and the bustle of the street around me began to muffle as if I was a plane flying through a cloud. I even started to see things too... because if I didn't know any better, I would swear that Leo was crossing the road towards the small scuffle that was taking place around me.

"Taylor, it is you?" he said, and it even sounded like him.

The two boys broke from their silent showdown to stare at him, and then at me. I was delayed in answering because I was still convinced that he was a figment of my imagination. Surely it wasn't him; surely he wasn't here.

"Taylor?" the Leo lookalike pressed.

"Taylor, I think he's talking to you," Brandon said, elbowing me. Harper edged forward at the gesture as if he might tear off Brandon's arm for making contact.

"Leo," I breathed. "You're here? You're really here?"

"*Si.*" He smiled. "And you are as beautiful as I remember."

I felt my cheeks blush as he reached out to cradle my cheek. "But how are you here?"

He shook his head. "The moment you left, I regretted letting you go. I wanted the chance to take you out properly."

"You're crazy," I sighed, feeling self-conscious. "*Pazzo.*"

He chuckled.

115

"Wow, wow, wow," Brandon interrupted. "Who is *this* guy?"

I couldn't tear my eyes from him, from fear that he would disappear.

"This is Leo Gatto," I explained. "Leo and I met in Italy."

"Italy?" Brandon repeated incredulously. "So, what is he doing here then?"

"He's… he's here to see me." I shrugged, peeling his hand off my cheek to hold.

Brandon cleared his throat. "You dated?"

"No, we never really got the chance," I replied. Leo smiled at me with his warm, glowing smile that I couldn't help but return.

"Right."

I glanced back to Brandon, and my smile faded. "Where did Harper go?"

"Who?" he asked.

"Harper."

"Taylor?" Leo said.

Brandon sighed. "I thought you had class anyway?"

"I…" I exhaled, and reached up for my head. "I think I might give classes a miss today."

"*Mi dispiace*," Leo murmured. "I am sorry to appear just like this."

I looked up at Leo and smiled. It felt forced.

"No, I'm glad you're here," I answered. "Why don't we go somewhere and sit?"

"*Sì*." Leo nodded.

116

Brandon looked offended, so I stopped. "Um, we'll catch up later, okay?"

"Whatever," he mumbled. "Apparently it's not important."

I drew in a breath as Brandon walked off, and I was quite sure that if Leo hadn't have slipped his hand into mine, I might have gone after him. I glanced back to the Italian man who had once stolen my heart, but all I could think about was Harper coming to my rescue, then disappearing, Brandon insisting on my attention, and then giving up, and the two of them walking away without even a hint of why they were seeking me out in the first place.

*

Having Leo in South Coast was a lot different to when we spent our time together in Italy. It wasn't better nor worse, it was just different. Maybe it was because now I was back in my world, the fantasy and fairy tales seemed a little harder to believe. Perhaps it was because, in Italy, it was just him and me, but now there was Brandon, and Harper, and I – and I didn't know what was happening with either of them.

Leo and I spent most of the morning catching up before we caught the bus to a hotel that was affordable, and close to town and transport. He was very understanding and patient with me, knowing that I would be preoccupied with uni, and was willing to suit my availabilities. In the meantime, he was going to busy himself with the sights of the city, and enjoy the holiday for as long as his money lasted for.

By the time I got home, I felt horrible, both physically and mentally. My head still pounded, so I took some paracetamol and went to lie down, even if the mental part would take a lot more than a painkiller. I felt terrible for what I had done to Brandon, not knowing to what extent I wanted to be with him. I felt conflicted by Harper because I felt something for him that I couldn't explain, and I wanted so badly to explore that. And then there was Leo who had travelled so far just to take me out on the date he'd longed for. Yet here I was caught between the guy I'd always wanted and the guy I wanted to know. It hardly seemed fair.

I dozed off stressing about the first world problems I was facing and woke to find the house in darkness. It was supposed to be spring, but for some reason, the rain clouds didn't want to leave. So, while the day started in sunshine, by mid-afternoon, it was blanketed in thick black clouds. It was eerie but somehow comforting, like a curtain shielding out the undesirable. I sat up and looked around for some sense of time, and saw it was after six o'clock. Jesse should be home, but it didn't appear like anyone else was here.

"Hello?" I called tentatively to the resounding silence. I usually didn't scare so easily being alone in the dark, but there was something menacing about the stillness that unsettled me. My feet felt unsteady as I stood, my head feeling too heavy for my shoulders, and I stumbled towards the lamp beside the television to at least shed some light on the room. It helped, but not much, so I turned the television on just for some noise to break the ghostly quiet.

I wandered into the kitchen for some water, and while I was there, ended up eating half the carton of yogurt straight from the container. The feeling I had of being watched seemed to get worse, and the paranoia I felt drove me to check all the locks on the doors and windows. After checking them all twice, I settled back on the couch and then nearly jumped out of my skin when Raven scooted out from underneath. I had only just calmed my erratic heartbeat when Jesse got home, and the sense of relief was tangible. We stayed up talking for a long time about our day, and he was interested to hear more about Leo, though, I was so exhausted, I think I fell asleep midsentence.

*

When I awoke the next morning in my bed, I felt a little more human having gotten some decent sleep. Jesse had left earlier but left porridge for me on the stove which I quickly ate before heading into uni. The day went slowly but was relatively uneventful, so for that, I couldn't complain. I tracked down one of the girls from the classes I missed the day before and got her notes, before heading to the library to catch up on the work.

"Hey, Taylor," April called as I crossed the courtyard.

I spun around, and I spotted her on one of the benches. She wasn't alone.

"Hey, April," I sighed. "Brandon."

"Taylor." Brandon nodded.

April shuffled closer towards him, his arm pinning her against his side. So, it seemed Brandon had moved on to greener, or keener, pastures.

"How are you?" April asked; though it sounded more like she was gloating, rather than actually interested in my wellbeing.

"Fine," I replied. "You?"

"Great." She grinned. "So we should catch up soon."

"Sure, April, yeah. I'll call you."

"Actually, why don't we make a time now?"

My eyebrows lifted. "Okay."

"What are you doing tomorrow night?" she asked.

"Uh, nothing I don't think." I shrugged.

"Great," she answered quickly. "I'll pick you up at seven."

I forced a smile. "Sure, I'll see you then."

April waved, and Brandon smiled as I turned and left. I continued back towards the library, then decided against it. I didn't want to be near this place any more. My phone rang, and I glanced at the caller ID.

"*Pronto,*" I said with a sigh. "*Ciao,* Leo."

"*Ciao, Taylor.*" He chuckled. "*When can I see you?*"

I stopped and looked at my watch. "How about now?"

"*Perfetto,*" he replied. "*Where will we meet?*"

"I'll come to you," I answered. "See you soon."

Leo was waiting out the front when I arrived, and I took him into the city to a little diner called *Lunar* for milkshakes.

"You seem different here," Leo noted, taking a sip of his chocolate milkshake. "Are you not happy being home?"

I played with my straw. "It's definitely not Italy."

"No, but it is your home."

I sighed. "Things are just different for me here now."

"In what way?" he asked. His Italian accent was beautiful; it made everything he said sound like poetry.

I thought for a moment, trying to verbalise the feeling.

"It just doesn't feel like home to me any more," I answered. "It doesn't feel safe, or familiar, or normal. I feel so out of place, like I don't recognise anything, you know."

Leo pressed his lips together. "You have seen much of the world, your eyes are open. It is not unusual that you feel out of place. You went through a *grande* change."

I nodded, but his words didn't comfort me.

"As for not feeling safe, I'm not quite sure what you mean," he said.

I frowned. "I um, just seem to be more accident prone since my return."

"Jet lag?"

"Probably." I shrugged dismissively, playing with my straw. It was easier than trying to explain my paranoia, though Harper seemed to understand it. A surge of guilt ran through me at the thought of him, and I couldn't help but feel like I was being dishonest for being here with Leo. It was irrational, but it was there.

"Smile, *bella*, Taylor." Leo grinned. "I will protect you."

I glanced up at him, and breathed a laugh, feeling more than Leo's pair of eyes on me – but it was a public place, so there was no reason why that meant anything sinister.

It was nice to spend time with Leo and reminisce about times when things seemed simpler, and I didn't feel so conscious about the prying eyes. By the time I got home, I felt a little more rested and ready to face the world again. Being with Leo made me want to live in my dream world, and it was a welcome distraction from all the seriousness that assaulted me upon my return.

Wednesday went too quickly, and after a couple of hours at the vet, I got myself organised for an evening with April. At a quarter-past seven, she arrived at my door with Brandon, and he stayed with Jesse while April and I headed out. It was strange seeing them together—probably not surprising when I thought about it—but I couldn't help but feel jealous of April. It was irrational, considering I had the opportunity to be with Brandon which I refused. But I guess I didn't think my refusal meant he'd give up; and no matter how selfish it was, I liked being desirable to him.

"So, I thought we'd go down to the foreshore and hang out like we used to," April explained as she drove. "We can grab fish and chips, and have a picnic just like old times."

I smiled tightly. "The foreshore sounds nice, but I don't really eat fried food any more."

"What? Lame."

"You're more than welcome to get some. I ate something earlier, so I'm okay."

"Yeah, and feel like a total pig eating all the *fried food* on my own." She groaned, rolling her eyes. I had to work not to roll mine.

We arrived at the river and positioned ourselves underneath a lamppost. It was fresh, but pleasant since there was hardly any breeze around due to the heavy cloud cover overhead.

"So," April sighed. She tapped her fingers on her knees impatiently, and then stood up. "Okay, I don't care. I'm starving, so I'm getting food."

"I said you could," I answered with a forced laugh.

"Whatever, I'll be back," she said, turning on her heel, and heading towards the fish and chip shop. I drew in a breath and sat back. It was going to be a long night.

"So, anyway, Brandon and I were like totally making out, and that librarian – you know the one who looks like a duck and who has probably never had a boyfriend in her life? Well, she caught us, and totally overreacted and threw us out, it was so embarrassing," April gushed as she picked at her chips. We'd been sitting for over an hour, and she was still making her way through the fatty meal which she laid out between us.

"Mm." I smiled.

"But I guess you had to be there," she sighed, half rolling her eyes. "So what's been up with you? That Italian guy flew out to see you, right? So, you two are, like, a couple?"

I opened my mouth, feeling a little offended by her offhanded tone. "No, not really. I mean, we've hung out a few times, but nothing serious."

"Uh-ha," she sighed.

I sat forward and hugged my knees, and April dusted her hands and stood up.

123

"I need to pee," she said.

I nodded and watched her walk towards the restrooms, and then gently closed my eyes. How long did I have to keep this up? Gosh, it was painful.

I listened to the sounds around me, wondering how much time had passed since April had left; at least five, possibly seven minutes. I looked over at the restroom block and frowned. Knowing my luck, she'd left me stranded here.

A few more minutes passed, and I began to get more squeamish. I glanced down at the remaining greasy fries beside me. If anything, April wouldn't leave these here. I chuckled at the thought and made myself a promise to find better friends. But for now, April was pretty much all I had. So, I stumbled to my feet, gathered the cold fries, and headed over to the restroom block, throwing the remains in the trash as I passed the bin.

"Hello?" I called, stepping into the dark block. "April?"

It was creepy; all I could hear was a dripping tap. Of course. This was how horror films began. I backed out and rounded the block, searching for a trace of my former best friend. I circled it twice, and found nothing, and was about to start frantic phone calls when I saw her pinned against the wall near the café kissing some strange guy.

I folded my arms and paced towards her.

"Um, April?" I sighed.

Her eyes shot open, and she pushed the guy away, wiping her mouth. "H-hey, Tay, I didn't see you there."

I shrugged. "Why would you? Your eyes were closed."

She gave a nervous laugh. "Right."

The guy she'd been kissing glanced at me, then slipped away. I didn't recognise him; all I knew is that he wasn't Brandon.

"What about Brandon?" I asked.

"I... that was nothing, just some guy I used to date," April answered breathlessly. "I mean, you don't need to tell Brandon, but it's not like we're exclusive."

"Right."

She rolled her eyes. "But you will, of course, because you want him for yourself."

"That's not... what is wrong with you? Are you *that* threatened by me that you feel the need to put me down all the time?"

She scoffed. "Oh please, you are so full of yourself, Taylor."

"Right, *I'm* full of *myself*." I groaned.

From the corner of my eye, I saw it, and I reacted quicker than I thought possible. The large metal sign of the café that was balanced above April wavered, falling loose from its fastening. I lunged towards her, dragging her down hard to the floor, the metal sheet barely missing us both. I heard a skin-crawling crunch, followed by April's blood-curdling squeal.

"Ah, my arm," she wailed. "What the hell, Taylor?!"

I sat back and caught my breath, starting at the two golden glowing dots in the blackness before glancing down at her disfigured arm.

"Sorry, the sign fell, and—"

"Ugh, I think it's broken," she panted. "Take me to the hospital, you klutz."

I exhaled and pushed myself up, then helped her to stand.

It was a long drive to the hospital, long and silent. I was quite convinced that whatever flicker of friendship that might have been between April and I had been hastily extinguished. I tried to mourn it but decided I didn't care. It was a liberating feeling.

We were closer to Iris Cove Private Hospital than South Coast Memorial Hospital, and since April grunted she had private health cover, I drove her there. I'd called Jesse on the way, and he met us at the emergency department and whisked her off right away. April told me to leave, but I stayed in the foyer to make sure that she was okay.

Brandon blew in a few minutes later after parking the car, flexing his disapproval. I didn't mention April and the random guy, I didn't feel it was the time.

An hour passed, then two. Jesse came out to update us that April's arm had a closed forearm fracture. It needed to be in a cast for four to eight weeks, and she was doing okay. She wanted to see Brandon but didn't want to see me.

Jesse guided Brandon into her room, and then returned to where I was. I could tell by the way his brow furrowed, the way his shoulders tightened, and the hard fall of his foot, that he was disapproving of me too. I folded my arms defensively, bracing myself for a fight.

"Why are you still here, Taylor?" he asked. "April said to go. She doesn't want to see you."

"As if I was going to leave," I sighed. "Jesse, I didn't do whatever April said."

He stole a sideways glance at me and pressed his lips together. So this was how it's going to be now. She was blacklisting me and poisoning my own brother against me.

"Jess, come on, it's me, you know me. I'm not openly vindictive," I answered. "Please."

His gaze dropped, and I heard him exhale. "Well, I wasn't about to believe you tackled and body-slammed her because you were jealous of her and Brandon."

"That's what she's claiming?"

Jesse smiled sardonically.

"There was a sign that fell off its hinges, and I pushed her out the way," I explained. "After I found her making out with some random ex of hers."

Jesse frowned. "Isn't she seeing Brandon?"

I shrugged. "Right."

"April is toxic and contagious."

"I need to speak to Brandon."

He was shaking his head before I'd finished talking. "All you need to do is go, and make sure she doesn't see you here."

"No, not until I talk to Brandon and explain," I replied, heading in the direction of April's room. Jesse caught my arm.

"Now is not the time," he said sternly. "And quite frankly, it's not your place to tell Brandon about what you may or may not have seen, it's April's. Just stay out of it, Taylor, I'm begging you."

I stared my brother in the eye, feeling the blood drain from my face.

"Don't you believe me?" I asked.

He released my arm. "That's not what I said."

"It's what you implied."

"Look, things have been weird with you since you got back," he answered. "Just don't go looking for trouble. You'll just cause unnecessary waves."

"Brandon is your friend. Don't you think he has a right to know if April is being unfaithful?"

Jesse looked at me with humour. "Have you met Brandon? Don't you think it goes both ways?"

I exhaled.

"Just go home, Taylor," he sighed. "Seriously."

"Fine," I mumbled.

I headed towards the door and stopped when I got outside. It was dark, and I didn't have a ride home since April had driven me in her car and demanded her keys back after I'd gotten her safely to the hospital. Luckily, home wasn't too far, but it would be a decent walk.

"Taylor." My name came from the darkness after ten minutes of foot treads.

I jumped and my breathing hitching in my throat. My hand rested on my beating heart as I searched for the source.

"Harper," I sighed.

He was on foot too; he stepped out of the shadow and into the limited light of the cloud-covered Waning Gibbous.

128

"Why are you out on your own?" he asked. "Didn't I tell you to try harder to take care?"

"I think I remember something to that degree," I replied. His eyebrows lifted expectantly, and I shrugged. "I was at the hospital, and I didn't have a ride. My house isn't far."

He nodded and stepped beside me, looking down at his feet. I started walking.

"You were at the hospital," he noted, tucking his hands deep in his navy jeans. "Not for you, I hope."

"No, unfortunately," I exhaled.

Harper glanced up at me with a curious look. "Unfortunately?"

"I would have preferred it to be me. It would have been easier."

"I don't quite follow."

"I sort of fractured April's arm."

He breathed a laugh. "I see."

"It wasn't intentional," I continued. "I was actually protecting her from this metal thing that was going to hit her. I kind of wish I'd have just let it fall on her now."

His smile faded. "It was going to hit her."

"Well, it was coming at us both, but I guess I panicked," I sighed. "Now everyone is mad at me, and Jesse thinks I'm crazy."

"You're not."

"I know."

We walked in comfortable silence for a while, and it dawned on me that I'd never received an explanation from him as to why he believed what everyone else called paranoia.

"Harper," I said quietly. His name sounded strange coming from my lips.

"Yes, Taylor," he replied.

I allowed myself to smile at the way he said my name, and then remembered my question. "What, um, what, why... um, you said you knew something when I was in the hospital. You never told me why I needed to be careful."

He smiled to himself. "I worry about you, Taylor."

My heart stuttered over a beat. "That's not an answer. Not really."

"I know."

We continued to walk, and I waited, sneaking a peek up at him when he didn't reply. After a moment, I cleared my throat. Harper looked troubled.

"It's quite hard to explain," he said thoughtfully. "And not something I'd prefer to discuss in the open."

My brow creased. "I don't understand."

"You will." He nodded. "I will tell you everything that I know."

Phase Six
The Death Sentence

Harper didn't say anything more about it until we reached my house, and as we walked up the driveway, I noticed I had company waiting for me.

"Leo is here," I whispered, glancing at Harper.

Harper's eyes narrowed. "He is... he is smitten with you."

"I'll... I'll get rid of him," I murmured. "So we can talk."

Harper nodded once, and I frowned up at Leo. When I looked back to my side, Harper had disappeared, materialised into the darkness as he did so well. I took a deep breath.

"Leo," I sighed. "Um, what are you doing here?"

"I come to see you," he answered with a smile, his fingers gently tucking his smooth brown hair behind his ear. "I needed to speak to you."

"Oh." I nodded. "Well, uh, maybe we should make a time—"

"This cannot wait," he interrupted, taking a step towards me.

I bit my lower lip, and he picked up my right hand and pressed it to his chest. I could feel the quick thud of his heart beneath it, the warmth of his body transferring through the soft material of his shirt. I discretely cleared my throat, feeling a little awkward. Where was Harper? Could he see us? Could he hear us?

"You make my heart race, Taylor," he said earnestly. "From the moment I set my eyes on you, I wanted to know you, and now that I do, I want to be with you."

I felt my eyebrows pull together in a pucker. I was not expecting this. "I, um…"

"Let me be with you," he whispered. "Say you will be mine, Taylor."

"I… I…"

Leo read my face, perhaps my worry and hesitation, and raised a finger to my lips.

"Don't answer now. You need to think," he said.

I nodded.

"Okay." He smiled, leaning in to kiss my forehead. "I will call you."

I opened my mouth to reply, and then realised my voice may still be MIA, so nodded again.

"*Buena notte, bella,*" he murmured, caressing my cheek as he left.

I turned and watched him go, staring at his shadow as it grew larger the further away he got. Leo was the man I should be with. He is everything that my parents would want me to be with, and would treat me better than a queen. So what was my problem? And why was it even a decision?

I jumped as Harper suddenly appeared beside me, and then tried to calm myself.

132

"Are you ready to go?" he asked.

I nodded and then frowned. "Wait, go where?"

Harper glanced up. "It is not safe here."

"What? Why? What do you mean?"

"Taylor, you need to trust me," he whispered. "I will explain everything. Just not here."

My shoulders slumped. "Not here. Then where?"

He raised his hand, his finger a gesture of silence. "Somewhere safe."

"Okay. Lead the way."

He pressed his lips together, and rested his warm fingers softly on my elbow, guiding me back down the driveway.

"I do, by the way," I murmured, looking over at him in the darkness. His olive eyes seemed to glow.

"Do what?" he asked.

"Trust you."

He looked down but didn't reply. I cleared my throat.

"So, where are we going?" I asked. "Are we walking there?"

"My bike isn't far," he answered.

"Bike?"

"Yes."

"I didn't pick you for a biker," I replied.

"I like to feel the speed I'm going," he said with a small smile.

"That's what my brother says," I murmured. "But he drives a convertible."

Harper's lips twitched, and I bit mine, feeling his hand rest lightly on my lower back. I liked it, it made me feel safe, protected. I smiled at the floor and nervously tucked my hair behind my ear.

"Just up here," he murmured, nodding towards the shadows. I could hardly make anything out until we got closer, and I saw the glistening metal in the distance.

We walked closer, and Harper's hand moved more protectively around me the darker our surroundings grew. His bike was crafted metal, appropriately branded *Shadow*. It was sleek and beautiful and utterly terrified me.

"After you," he murmured, gesturing to the black leather seat.

I blinked. "You... you want me to sit on the front?"

"You are smaller than me." He smirked. "I will protect you from anything that might threaten you."

"While I'm on the bike?"

"Please, Taylor."

Any hesitation I felt melted away. I climbed over the seat, positioning myself behind the handlebars, and waited as Harper slid on behind me. He nudged me forward, and leant over, the warmth of his chest burning through my sweater. He plugged in the key, and revved it to life, spinning swiftly out of the darkness, and into the light rimmed streets. We were going fast, almost too fast, and I was chilled by the cold night air that whipped by us. My body convulsed in a shiver, and Harper hunched closer. I took the opportunity to snuggle into his hold. I felt safe.

I barely registered where we were; I was too preoccupied with the steady thud of Harper's heart against my back, and the even breathing that fanned my neck.

He spun into a dark car park, then through some high cast-iron gates, and then noticeably slowed. I looked around at the headstones and swallowed.

"Tell me this is not your safe place," I called, turning my head. I was startled to find his face so close, and his perfect olive-green eyes were peering down at me.

"The cemetery is the safest place for you now," he answered. "There is no reason to fear the dead, only the living dead."

My mouth fell open in confusion, then snapped closed as he made a sharp turn to what looked like a built-up tomb. It was older, and more worn than the other structures around the graveyard, and somehow gave me more chills than the simple headstones and angels that stared at us.

"Come," he murmured, climbing off the seat, and offering me his hand. I took it without thinking, and let myself be led inside the dark, vine-riddled tomb. Harper's hand slipped free from mine when we were inside, moving into his pocket to retrieve a lighter, and then he began lighting the almost stubbed candles scattered around the inside.

"Harper, what are we doing here?" I asked, warming my arms. "What's going on?"

It had only just occurred to me that I had unknowingly got on the back of a near stranger's bike, and was now standing in the middle of a deserted cemetery with said stranger with no explanation.

Harper turned and extinguished the lighter, replacing it in his pocket.

"As I said, here is the safest place for you now," he replied. "What's hunting you cannot tread on holy ground."

My eyes squeezed shut and I shook my head. "What's hunting me? I'm being hunted? By what?"

"For me to explain so you will believe me, I fear I need to start from the beginning."

"The beginning? I don't understand."

"The night you arrived home," he continued. "The drive back from the airport. You heard something, something that gave you those scratches on your back."

I numbly reached around to feel my healing shoulder. "Right, but what does that have to do—?"

"Because that night you were marked."

"Marked? By what?"

"By death. By a banshee."

I breathed a humourless laugh. "Banshee, what is this? An episode of *Charmed*? *Supernatural*?"

His head tipped. "Did you not think it strange that all of a sudden you were so accident prone? That strange things keep happening to you? Almost as if you were a magnet for misfortune?"

My mouth opened and then closed again. Harper stayed silent as I let the idea, the crazy concept, sink in.

"How do you know all this?" I asked. "And what does my wellbeing have to do with you?"

He looked down. "I guess I feel responsible for you."

"Why?"

"Because it should have been me," he answered, glancing up at me with his piercing stare. "You saved my life at your own expense."

"I don't follow."

"It was me," he whispered, peeling off his jacket. I took a step back as he gripped the bottom of his black singlet and pulled it over his head. His hand rested on his right shoulder, and he turned to reveal a faint pink line down his shoulder blade. I took a step closer to get a better look, half distracted by the incredible body that had been pressed against mine not ten minutes ago.

"You?" I said, reaching out to trace the line. I glanced up at his eyes as they watched me intently, those eyes that seemed so familiar, the colour that I'd only seen once before...

Recognition hit me like a force of freak lightning.

"No," I breathed. "No..."

"Yes." He nodded. "I am a wolf, Taylor. It was me that night that you saved from death, and now it's my job to return that favour."

"But... I... how... what?" I stuttered. "No, that's not possible."

"Not even the slightest bit possible?" he asked, his eyebrows lifting. "Not possible that you drew a silver dagger from my shoulder blade that night, moments before hearing a scream that smashed your brother's car windows?"

I blinked. "How did you…?"

"Because I was there," he sighed, pulling his singlet back over his head.

"Because you're a wolf?" I clarified. "Like a werewolf?"

"People call us that, sure."

"Okay."

"You think I'm lying?"

I shook my head. "I don't know what to think."

He folded his arms. "It's a lot to accept."

"So this thing that's after me is a banshee?"

"No," he answered. "The banshee just marked you, they do not necessarily kill. They often send other creatures on their behalf. What's after you is much worse."

"Of course." I chuckled. "So what is it? A vampire? Boogieman? A… wendigo?"

"Yes." He nodded. "It's a wendigo."

"I was kidding."

"You shouldn't joke about this, it's rather serious," he said solemnly. "It's hunting you. It's been hunting you from that night."

I looped around and sat on the edge of a ledge. The dampness was cold on my jeans, but I didn't care. Harper was silent, letting his words settle, and I rested my head in my hands, rubbing my forehead delicately. He was a wolf – the wolf that I'd helped. I had been marked with death by a

138

screaming banshee, and now a wendigo was after me. Harper was here to make sure that I lived because I had saved his life.

I straightened and looked up at him. He was observing me.

"I saved your life," I murmured.

"Yes." He nodded. "Thank you. I don't think I've ever said it."

I shook my head. "Wait, that's why you're here?"

"To protect you. Yes, Taylor, as I said."

"But that's it? There's no other reason?"

"I'm not sure what you mean."

I cleared my throat. "I mean, that's the only reason why you're… why you've been seeing me? To watch over me?"

His pressed his lips together and I let out a pathetic sigh, dropping my head back in my hands. I felt like an idiot. All this time I'd been swooning over him, and batting my eyes at him, all he wanted was to make sure I wasn't going to die. It was mortifying. I wanted to hide or eat chocolate until I felt sick. I wanted to disappear. My ears were pounding loudly with my erratic heartbeat, so I didn't hear Harper walk towards me, but his hand was suddenly on my shoulder, and I gasped.

"I'm sorry," he whispered, noting my fright. "And I'm sorry that I gave you the wrong impression, but I'm not boyfriend material. I'm not good for you. I'd be more likely to tip the scales in fate's favour."

"So, why are you here then?" I asked.

"Because right now, I'm your best chance at surviving this thing," he replied. "I will protect you, Taylor. Then I promise I will disappear forever."

Pain stabbed in my chest at the thought, but it was unreasonable. He was never mine, as much as I had wanted him to be, and he just said that his only reason for being around me was a matter of life and death. No matter what, when this was over, I had to sever all ties with Harper. Regardless of how he made me feel, regardless of how much I wanted to know him. I needed to let it go and focus on healthier pastimes... like work, and study, and exercise. When this was over before it had a chance to really begin.

"So, the night of the uni party... you knew who I was," I said. "Were you following me?"

He shook his head. "No, I was just there... I had just changed back. The Full Moon, the day before, and the day after, they affect me still. I did not know who you were for sure until you showed me your shoulder. I recognised you, and you told me about the things that were happening to you, but I was still hoping that you weren't affected by that night – that you hadn't been marked."

I took even breaths. "So, what does this mean?"

"It means you're in danger. The banshee marks those intended for death. That night it was supposed to be me, but you intervened. Now it's you that fate is after."

"Fate?" I asked. "Not the wendigo?"

"The wendigo is fulfilling that fate," he explained. "Just like the universe has been sending other things your way."

"The wasps, the spider, freak falling signs..."

"Right."

I sighed. "So, what's the plan then?"

"For now, you need to stay here," he replied, standing up and beginning to pace.

"And for later? I can't stay here forever."

Harper nodded.

I frowned. "Or my forever, which may or may not be a long time."

"No, nothing is happening to you," he answered defiantly, shaking his head. "Even if I need to call for help to hunt this thing."

"Hunt it? How long is that supposed to take?" I asked. "Because I have classes, and people are going to notice that I'm missing."

"You do understand that your life is in danger, do you not?" he clarified, pulling a black object out of his pocket. He dialled without looking at it and raised it to his ear. "Hunter; I need you. Amund Tomb. I'll explain when you get here."

He hung up the phone and exhaled.

"Who's Hunter?" I asked. "Another werewolf?"

He glanced up at me. "Not quite. She's a friend."

She. Jealousy pricked at me; I drew in a breath and let it out. "What about Leo?"

"Leo?" he repeated. "The Italian?"

I narrowed my eyes. "Yes."

"What about him?"

"I need to talk to him. He asked me a question earlier, and he's expecting my answer."

Harper rubbed his forehead. "Taylor, he... he... he'll have to wait."

"But—"

"You've been marked by death, Taylor!"

"What does that even mean? I can't date?"

"It means you need protecting," he answered sternly. "And while he may be capable in protecting you from... from some things, he's not the one for it on this occasion."

My eyebrows lifted. "What does that mean? What are you saying? That you are?"

He exhaled. "I can protect you if you just let me."

"A few days ago you didn't want me *near* you, and now you want to *protect* me?" I asked. "I wish you'd make your mind up what you want from me."

"I can't... Please, Taylor."

"No. I'm not doing this, I'm not. I like Leo, he could be good for me, and unlike some, *he's* not emotionally unavailable."

Harper's mouth popped open. "That's..."

My eyebrows lifted. "What? That's what?"

Harper took a deep breath and let it out in frustration. "I have already told you that I'm no good for you."

"Right. So let me have this. Let me at least *try* and be happy with someone else."

"This isn't about being happy, Taylor. I want you to be happy," he whispered. "I also want you to be safe and *alive*."

My head was shaking crossly. "So, how long is this going to go on for? Forever? When can I start living my own life then Harper?"

"I don't know," he answered angrily, and then closed his eyes. "I don't know, Taylor. Just give me a few days to get this thing, and then you can be with the Italian, or whoever. Just at least give me that much. I need to try."

"A few hours. No more."

"Taylor, the Full Moon cycle begins Friday; that's less than two days. I *need* a Full Moon to—"

"That's my best offer. Take it or leave it."

"I am not doing this to hurt you," he answered. "We all need to make sacrifices, Taylor. The choice is yours. You can go now and hedge your bets, or just stay here with me and let me give you your life back."

I frowned. "If what you're saying is true – if this thing is after me and I am marked, what's to stop something else coming after me when it's gone?"

"One problem at a time," he whispered.

"Harper," a female voice interrupted; and in walked a goddess-looking girl with sleek dark brown hair, and Mediterranean skin. She was, perhaps, the most stunning girl I'd ever seen in person. My self-esteem drained as quickly as the blood in my face.

"Hunter," he sighed. "Thanks for coming."

Her dark brown eyes traced to me. "Who is the girl?"

"She's the one who saved me," Harper said, nodding towards me as he folded his arms. His brow cast a shadow over his eyes.

Hunter's eyebrows lifted. "*She's* the one? What is she still doing alive then?"

I frowned at the brunette beauty, her Spanish accent was becoming more hostile by the second.

Harper scoffed. "I plan on keeping her that way. That is why I need your help."

"Risk my life to keep her alive?" she asked in disdain. I groaned, and her head snapped in my direction. "Problem, human?"

"Put the claws away, Hunter," Harper warned.

"I beg your pardon?" I asked. "Who are you?"

"Hunter is an old friend," Harper said. "She's a shifter, a panther, she can help."

"Harper!" Hunter hissed.

I rolled my eyes. "And here I thought you weren't a cat person, Harper."

His lips twitched.

"I did not come here to be mocked," she snarled. "Her feeble human life is not *my* problem."

"Is my life?" Harper asked.

"Yours? Why?"

"Because there is a wendigo after her, and I plan to take it down," he explained. "I can do it by myself, but I'd prefer to have backup."

Hunter shook her head. "You cannot take a wendigo down solo. I do not even know if you *and* I can take a wendigo down. They're strong, too strong, and their human form is a tough match for a feline or canine."

Harper frowned. "You're not suggesting...?"

Hunter shrugged. "If there is any hope in defeating this thing, we might have to call them."

"Call who?" I asked. "Who? More werewolves?"

Harper shook his head. "As far as I know, I'm the only one in South Coast."

He looked at Hunter who shrugged. "If you do not involve them, the girl might not die, but we will."

"It's not their fight," he murmured, beginning to pace again. "But you're right."

"Who?" I groaned. "Who are you talking about?"

Harper looked up. "The vampires."

"Hold up. Vampires? There are *vampires* in South Coast?"

"There are vampires everywhere. They're a little easier to miss since they don't morph into panthers or violent hounds by moonlight."

"But they turn to dust in the sun," I replied, and then tacked on. "Don't they?"

Hunter breathed a laugh, but Harper was shaking his head.

"Not real vampires," he answered. "Real—"

"*Real* vampires." I scoffed.

Harper smirked. "Well, they weaken in the sun, but it is more excessive dehydration until they are as good as dead. Any sort of heat is bad for vampires, so they tend to stay indoors."

"Right," I sighed. "So, who are these vampires you're calling in?"

"Some I met when I first came here, he used to run the bar *Crescent* in town, but now she does, the newer one. The other female comes and goes."

145

"But aren't vampires and werewolves supposed to hate each other?" I asked.

Hunter made another noise of amusement. "Gullible one, isn't she?"

Harper shot her a look of warning but otherwise ignored her. "Why would we hate each other? Because mythology says so?" he replied with a knowing smile. "We are collectively different, yet collectively mythological. Our greatest allies are those that know our secret and those that can keep that from the humans."

My eyebrows lifted. "So, I'm the enemy?"

"If the shoe fits." Hunter shrugged.

"You are the exception to the rule." Harper smiled. "The only exception."

Hunter rolled her eyes. "Are we doing this? I have plans."

Harper sighed. "Hunter, so eager to hunt?"

"Eager to finish what *she* started," Hunter replied, nodding in my direction.

"*She* did not start this. If you are not with Taylor, you are no help to me. I may not have much of a chance on my own, but I have more of a chance fighting this thing by myself with the vampires, than with a cat with no allegiance."

Hunter hissed. "Did I say I would not help? No matter my feelings towards the human, I will not sit idly by and watch your suicide mission."

"Then we have an understanding."

Hunter glanced over at me and lowered her head in a nod.

146

"Call the vampires already, Lovett," she said. "I am getting bored."

Not four minutes had passed since Harper had hung up the phone there were two additions to our hunting party, a male and a female. Beautiful and flawless, the two vampires carried themselves, both pale and blonde in their glory, making me feel more and more insecure as a human. Both looked like runway models with trendy clothes and styled hair. Their keen silver eyes took in the severe expressions of the shifters, and then the awed look that must've been on my face. It was the male who spoke. He stepped forward to shake Harper's hand as if they were old friends. I fleetingly wondered how old.

"Thank you for coming, Cole." Harper nodded. "Ruby."

"You called, friend, we are here," Cole replied, glancing at his companion. "What is the emergency?"

Harper swallowed and glanced back at me. I straightened, and then stumbled over a stone at my foot. Hunter scoffed.

"Cole, Ruby, this is Taylor," Harper explained. "She was kind enough to come to my assistance last Full Moon when I had been wounded by silver. It came at a cost though, and unfortunately, she has been marked by a banshee."

Cole's eyes lifted towards me. "A banshee? Are you sure?"

Harper turned in my direction. "Show him the scratches."

I bit my lip and peeling back the fabric of my top over my left shoulder. Cole flittered towards me in the blink of an eye, and I gasped. He smiled apologetically as he glanced at the mark.

"Sorry," he murmured, pressing a cold finger to the graze. "Hm, yes."

I let the fabric go, and adjusted it back into place.

"You are brave." Cole nodded. "Most would not stop to help a wounded wolf."

I shrugged. "I'm training to be a vet."

"Still." He smirked. "I've been studying humans for a while now, and let me tell you, most would not stop."

"Yes, yes, she is amazing," Hunter grumbled. "She is also dead if we do not do something to shake the wendigo that's on the prowl."

"Wendigo?" the female vampire Ruby asked. "In South Coast?"

"Are you sure?" Cole frowned.

Harper nodded. "I have been tracking it since it caught Taylor's scent."

"What exactly is a wendigo?" I asked. I had heard the name before, but couldn't remember the characteristics of the supernatural monster that sets it apart from the others.

The four creatures around me exchanged uneasy looks.

"What?" I breathed.

Harper stepped forward. "A wendigo is perhaps the most heinous and grotesque of monsters, and poses the biggest threat to humans."

"Like vampires, they were once human," Cole continued, pacing around the slab of the tomb that divided the room. "Humans who turn cannibalistic, resulting in acquired superhuman qualities, such as extreme speed, and strength."

148

"But, unlike vampires, they have not experienced death themselves," Ruby added. "But are similarly undead in nature."

Hunter sighed. "This makes them hard to kill, and hard to track. See, the thing is, since they are technically still alive, they tend to blend. It's the night when they often attack, appearing only as shining eyes in the shadows."

I cleared my throat. "Gold... golden eyes?"

"You've seen it?" Harper asked through clenched teeth.

I shrugged. "I've sort of felt like I was being watched since that night. When you said you were following me, I assumed it was you."

"No."

"It's not a good sign if it's allowing itself to be seen," Cole said. "It's going to strike."

"So, what happens when you get this wendigo?" I asked. "You kill it, then what?"

Harper frowned. "What do you mean?"

"I mean, as long as I'm marked, I'm on someone's hit-list, right?" I replied. "This thing is probably one in a long line of things that will come after me."

"One problem at a time, Taylor," Harper sighed dismissively.

"Stop doing that, Harper!" I exclaimed. "This is my life you're talking about."

"She's right," Cole answered. "And to answer your question, Taylor, I fear the only way to *take you off the hit-list* as you put it, is to kill the banshee that marked you."

"Kill death?" Hunter huffed. "Is that even possible?"

"I agree with Harper, one thing at a time," Ruby said politely. "So, where do we go from here? I gather we're going to have to divide into hunting teams? Do we know where it's been basing itself? Cole, am I right in saying they often have a sort of lair?"

Cole nodded. "Yes, and that's probably the best way to go about it. Harper, do you know where it's been staying?"

Harper frowned. "It's been trailing Taylor pretty close, but if I had to hazard a guess, I would say it is somewhere around her apartment."

I shivered. Jesse.

"Then we'll start there and branch out," Cole said. "Harper, since it's not a Full Moon for another couple of days, you'll have to stay with either Ruby or me just in case."

"What about Taylor?" Ruby asked.

"She will be safe here," Harper murmured.

"Not on her own? Is that wise?"

"The wendigo cannot cross holy ground," Cole answered. "She will be safe if she stays here."

I exhaled. "Then I'm going to need some things. If I'd have known I'd be locked in a cemetery, I would have packed an overnight bag or something."

Cole and Ruby glared at Harper.

"You didn't get her to bring anything?" Cole frowned.

Harper shrugged. "I was on my bike, and I was more concerned about getting her out of there."

"Granted." Cole nodded. "Okay, Hunter, you go—"

"No," Hunter and I answered in unison. We looked at each other, and then looked away.

"I'd like to get my own things," I replied.

"No, out of the question," Harper said defiantly. "It's not safe."

"Harper, please, you can even come with me," I sighed, walking towards him. "I just need some creature comforts to make this feel a little less like I'm living in a tomb… starting with a blanket."

I shivered, and he reached out to rub my shoulders.

"It won't be for long," he whispered. His eyes were entrancing, and I momentarily forgot we had an audience.

"Ruby will take Taylor," Cole said. "She's stronger than you right now Harper, and has a car."

I looked up. "What about Jesse? What if he comes home?"

"Isn't he at the hospital?" Harper frowned.

I shrugged. "He was."

"Who's Jesse?" Hunter asked.

"My twin brother."

"Enter through the back window, and try and be quiet," he sighed. "It's not so much for him seeing you or Ruby than explaining why you need an overnight bag."

"Isn't it better that he does see me?" I said. "He'll worry if I just disappear."

"She's right." Ruby nodded. "We'll have enough on our plates without harbouring a missing person. If her brother is home, she'll tell him she's staying with a friend, if not, she'll leave a note."

151

I bit my lip. "Uh, one problem. I don't really… have a lot of friends at the moment. See, I just go back from Europe, and after recent events, my one friend isn't really talking to me."

Hunter laughed. "Perfect."

"Quiet, Hunter," Harper warned. "Taylor, is there anyone Jesse would believe you might stay with?"

"Maybe someone he doesn't know?" Cole added.

I glanced between them and shrugged. "Well, the only person really I can think of mentioning to him that he doesn't know is… is you, Harper."

"Won't be too hard to lie about spending time with him since it's sort of true," Ruby answered.

I thought about what my brother might say if I tell him I'm spending a few days with Harper. It would no doubt get back to Brandon, and therefore April; and what happens if word was to reach Leo? After he professes his desire, I up and spend time with another guy?

"We're losing moonlight," Cole said. "Ruby, you take Taylor to get some things. Keep to the lit areas, and don't let her out of your sight. If you hear or see anything, get her out of there fast and by any means necessary. Harper, Hunter, and I will start planning out routes to cover."

"No, I'm going with them," Harper replied. "Two sets of eyes and ears are better than one."

Hunter sighed. "Harper, for goodness sake—"

"No!" he exclaimed. "I started this, I am the reason Taylor is in danger. I want to ensure that she survives this."

Cole exhaled. "Fine. Twenty minutes, that's all you've got."

152

"Then let's not waste it." Ruby nodded.

Phase Seven
The Hunted

Jesse wasn't home when we arrived, which I was glad about, but equally as disappointed. Maybe it was the way that Cole had swept Ruby into his arms before we left, and kissed her so passionately before telling her to be careful, that made me realise the danger I was in. Or maybe it was the build-up of the last few weeks and, at last, an explanation for them all. Regardless, I was quite sure that if the four supernatural strangers couldn't conquer the dangerous creature that thirsted for me, I would be dead.

"In and out in no more than seven minutes, Taylor," Ruby said from the window of the black Jag she drove. She had parked on the back street which made up the back perimeter of my block. It was darker, so we'd escape human eyes, but I knew now that darkness meant little to the wendigo. "I'll keep watch out here. Harper, you give her a hand," Ruby finished quietly. Her words weren't demanding, but they were firm.

I liked Ruby, she seemed to be more in touch with my feelings than the others, but maybe that was because she remembered what it was like to be human.

Harper and I hurried into the shadow-dwelling house, and after two unsuccessful attempts to get the door unlocked, his hands swept in and opened it for me.

"Five minutes," he murmured. "Bring only the essentials."

I nodded in reply, not trusting my voice for one second. My heart was in a sprint to the point that it muffled my hearing. I darted to my room, and pulled out my uni bag, emptying the contents on the bed before beginning to stuff supplies in it.

"For goodness sake, Taylor, do not make it look like you are in a frantic rush," Harper sighed, noting the crap on my mattress.

I looked up incredulously. "You give me five minutes to pack for I-don't-know-how-long, and you're worried it will *look* like I was in a rush?"

He exhaled, waving his hand. "Keep going."

I shook my head and jammed another sweater into my bag, along with one of my uni books from the messy pile, and headed into the bathroom. I wasn't sure if water would be readily available, but I figured since Harper was trying to keep me alive, it would be. I grabbed my toothbrush and toothpaste, floss, deodorant, perfume, eyeliner, and a pocket mirror, and stuffed it in the bag. I crouched down to retrieve a bottle of antibacterial gel that I knew was in the cabinet under the sink and gasped as a sharp pain shot up my right hand as I opened the door.

"Harper! Snake!" I panted, falling onto my back as the serpent slithered behind me out the bathroom door. I glanced back and saw Harper's foot clamp down on the reptile, his hand enclosing around its neck as he stepped past me to the bath, and severed its head.

He muttered something unintelligible under his breath and dropped the dagger he held – the same dagger I'd pulled from his shoulder that first night. He shook his blistered hand, finding one of Jesse's socks to tie securely around the bite, and used another one to fasten firmly around my wrist.

"Try not to move, that snake was poisonous," he murmured urgently. "We need to leave now. Cole will need to get some anti-venom from the hospital. How does that feel? Not too tight?"

I shook my head, gasping, and he rested a hand on my chest.

"Try and calm yourself, or the venom will spread faster," he said.

"Right, easy," I breathed.

Harper reached back to pick up the dagger with a hand towel and pushed it into my bag. He zipped it and draped it over his shoulder.

"I'm going to lift you up, try not to move your hand," he whispered. "Rest it in your lap."

"Okay."

Harper slid his hands under my knees and around my back, lifting me as if I was no heavier than a pillow. He moved quickly, without jostling me at all, towards the door, and managing to pull it silently closed behind him.

"I am so sorry, Taylor," he whispered. "I should not have left you alone."

I breathed a laugh. "You weren't to know there'd be a snake under my sink."

Ruby flittered out the car and opened the door for him. "What happened?"

"Snakebite, call Cole, we need anti-venom urgently," he answered. "Tell him it bit her on the hand, and it was a tiger snake."

"Tiger snake." Ruby groaned. "Harper."

"I know," he muttered. "Drive, Ruby."

The car wheels spun with the scent of burnt rubber, and we were speeding down the dark road.

"Any trace of the wendigo?" Harper asked, cradling my head, his hand enclosing over mine.

"No," Ruby answered. "I caught its scent, I think, but it wasn't fresh."

Harper nodded and began debriefing Cole in quick, clipped sentences as his voice sounded through the car speakers.

"How does Cole get the anti-venom from the hospital?" I asked airily. It felt like someone was pressing down hard on my ribcage, and I could feel beads of sweat begin to form on my forehead.

"He is a doctor," Harper whispered. "He used to work at South Coast Memorial."

I frowned. "My father works there."

"Shh. I know."

"I feel nauseous."

"We're almost back at the cemetery," he said, brushing my forehead. My eyes began to droop, my muscles felt fatigued. I wondered if this was what it felt like to die. I suppose given current circumstances, it was one of the better ways to go.

"Cole's going to get some and meet us back in five minutes. How's she doing?" Ruby asked.

"Not great, she's losing consciousness," Harper sighed, his beautiful French-English accent sounding worried. My eyes rolled, and I let out a couple of pathetic sounding coughs, then welcoming the darkness that had been threatening me.

My hand felt cold, and I struggled to open my eyes to deduce the reason behind it. I heard mutterings, and Harper sounded like he was unhappy about something.

"Stop, Cole, you are taking too much," he mumbled. "She has recently had a transfusion."

"The anti-venom will be more effective if it hasn't spread as far through her system," Cole explained. The coldness had disappeared, and I felt something sharp in my arm. "Her blood only has small traces. She needs to rest, and she'll be fine."

"Thanks, Doc," Harper sighed.

I stopped struggling to open my eyes and let them stay closed. I could feel the rhythmic stroke of a warm hand on my head and allowed myself to drift away. This darkness felt safe.

When I awoke, I had no concept of time. But I was comfortable, too comfortable for the rocky, cold surroundings. I looked around sleepily, and the memories began to return with each blink. I was in danger, I was in a tomb, I went to collect some things, and was bitten by a snake. Harper and

Ruby drove me away, and then voices began fussing over me. I stretched out my left hand, feeling the layers of blanket beneath me; while I was out, they must have made a bed for me here.

"You are awake," Harper's voice said. "How do you feel?"

"Tired," I replied, then tried to lift my arms. "Achy."

"Cole said that's expected," he answered. "You had us all worried."

I smiled. "Can't get rid of me that easy."

"I would never try."

I tried to sit up, and he moved towards me.

"You need to rest," he said.

"I thought I'd been doing that," I sighed. "Where are the others?"

Harper grabbed a bottle of water from a nearby ledge. "Hunting. Are you thirsty?"

"Mm." I nodded.

He twisted the cap and helped me sip.

"Why are you here?" I asked.

"Someone had to take care of you."

"I thought you'd want to go out and get that thing."

"I do." He chuckled. "But you are my first priority."

"Why? You've already saved my life more than once. You don't owe me any more."

Harper looked down, tracing two healing bee stings on my left forearm.

"You asked me earlier if watching over you was the only reason why I've been seeing you," he murmured. "I would like to say that it is the only reason, but I would be lying."

159

I frowned. "I'm not sure what you mean."

He looked up and rolled his olive coloured eyes. "It is not the only reason why I have been seeing you, that is merely a bonus for me."

I bit my lip, and he smiled.

"The night of the party when we first met in human form," he said. "Your openness enthralled me. You didn't know me, but you opened your mind to me, and this is after you had saved my life."

"But?"

He frowned. "But what?"

"But you're not good for me," I said, using his earlier words. "You're not boyfriend material."

"No, I'm not, and it's wrong of me to humour the thought."

"Wrong for whom?"

"You," he whispered.

His eyes dropped to my lips, then returned to pierce my eyes. My breath caught in my throat, and he looked away.

"You should, uh, drink this," he said, reaching for a bag. I pulled myself up and leant back on the pillow propped against the wall. Harper pulled out a purple bottle and unscrewed the lid. "You only need a mouthful."

"What is it?"

"Colloidal silver," he replied. "It will protect you from many of the mythical things around here."

"Are there really that many?" I asked. "Surely South Coast isn't—"

"Taylor, please. It is not a question, it is a necessity. Drink it."

I took a swig and swallowed it. It tasted like rusty water. "Ugh. What's in it?"

"Silver." He smirked.

"Doesn't silver hurt you?" I frowned.

Harper looked down at his hand. It was still slightly pink.

"Yes," he replied.

"So, why—?"

"I don't want to hurt you, Taylor," he answered. "It's just a precaution."

I handed the bottle back to him, and he resealed it.

"You said many mythical things," I continued. "Does silver hurt vampires and wendigos too?"

He put the bottle back in the bag. "Vampires, yes. Wendigos, no."

"Do you think the vampires would hurt me?" I frowned.

"No. Not on purpose."

That reminded me.

"What happened when I was out?" I asked. "I heard you fussing over my transfusion or something?"

He glanced up. "By the time we got back here, the venom had spread some. Cole was not sure if the anti-venom would be able to fully expel the effect of the venom from your system."

I lifted my hand to examine it, but it was bandaged.

"Cole tried to suck some of it out," he explained. "I was worried he would take too much. You have already lost some blood this week."

"He drank my blood?" I asked.

"He was cleansing it of the venom, but yes."

I frowned.

"Are you okay?" Harper asked.

"That's a good thing," I replied, and Harper's eyebrows lifted. I rolled my eyes. "I mean, if my blood had silver in it before, it might have been too late. He did what was best, using what he had."

Harper nodded. "That is true. But I don't plan on putting you in that position again."

"You didn't plan on it the first time."

Harper tried to hide a smile, but failed, and then shook his head.

"So what about this Italian guy?" he asked. The change of subject caught me a little off guard.

"Who, Leo?" I sighed. "What about him?"

"You met him from your travels."

"Yes, I met him when I was in Italy. On one of my last days."

He smiled crookedly. "Such is fate."

I frowned. "Yes."

"So, he came to South Coast... to finally take you out properly."

"How did you...?" I whispered. "How long have you been following me?"

"You are quick. I'll give you that." He grinned and then turned serious. "But you should exercise some caution with him."

"Harper," I murmured.

He confused me completely. What was his game? Had he known of me when I was in Europe? What was the reason for him returning to South Coast? He'd never answered my question when I asked his purpose for returning. What was he doing that fateful night he was daggered by the side of the highway?

Harper looked up at me, not saying anything, letting my thoughts run away from me.

"Harper, why did you return to South Coast?" I asked.

He continued to look at me, letting the silence linger, and then looked down. "I told you, my godfather lives here."

"Is that the real reason?" I pressed. "Or is there another reason?"

"What other reason?"

I bit my lip. "Did you know me when I was in Europe?"

He glanced up. "We never met, but I knew of you. I saw you once on the train from Paris back to Rome. It was a week or so before you were due back, I later discovered. I was there that night at the café when you met him—the Italian—a minute or so later, and it would have probably been me paying for your gelato."

I frowned, feeling tears pinch behind my eyes. Harper? In Italy?

"I wish I'd have met you then," I whispered. Whispering was safe because my voice couldn't crack with the emotion I was choking on.

"But you met him," Harper answered. "He's probably better for you; he's human, at least. He will not threaten to hurt you every Moon cycle."

"But what if he's not the one I want?"

"You wouldn't be talking about the guy with the silver ute, would you?"

"Brandon?" I said and then laughed. "No."

He frowned. "That's too bad."

"Why do you say that? Why are you so convinced that you're not good for me?"

Harper's eyes locked on mine, and I barely remembered the words I had just spoken. His eyes seemed to twinkle with different shades of pale green. He blinked slowly, and a smile spread across his face. A beat passed, and he tipped his head, one of his eyebrows rising with the motion.

"Such is fate," he replied, and then sat back from me.

My mouth opened to reply, but before I could utter any words, the tomb door burst open, and there stood Hunter and Ruby. Ruby's blonde hair was pulled back in a braid, her envious body dressed in tight black clothes – perfect for flitting in the shadows. Hunter, on the other hand, had her hair out, windswept, and was pulling on a loose white t-shirt which appeared to be cut short to bare her midriff.

"Hey," Hunter said in an exhale. "What's going on?"

Harper smiled weakly at me, then turned his attention to the girls. "Anything?"

"Cole called and told us to meet back here," Ruby replied. "How are things here? Taylor, you're looking better."

"I feel a bit better." I nodded. "Thank you."

Ruby smiled, and Cole blew in the door.

"Hi," he sighed.

"Well?" Harper asked.

"The trail Ruby caught scent of near Taylor's house is old," he replied. "I tracked it out to some veterinary hospital, and then loop around by SCU."

Harper's jaw hardened. "Nothing new?"

Cole shook his head. "Not that I could fathom. Unless it got wiser and found a way to mask its scent."

Hunter folded her arms. "So what now? We let the girl go? Wait for it to show its face?"

Harper's head snapped up. "No! Taylor is not bait!"

Ruby and Cole exchanged a look that Harper missed.

"What then, Lovett?" Hunter asked. "She lives in a tomb forever? The spiders and scorpions will kill her first."

"Scorpions?" I yelped.

"There are no scorpions here," Ruby whispered to me.

I swallowed, and Harper stood up, pacing the length of the small room.

"There's got to be another way... another place to look," he said. "It cannot have just disappeared; its mission is not yet complete."

I shivered and then shook my head. "Hunter is right."

"What?" Harper near growled.

I sat back, startled by the wild look on his face. "I mean, I can't stay here forever. Why don't I just perch somewhere under your watch and, you know, smoke the thing out?"

165

Hunter, Cole, and Ruby all looked to Harper for his reaction, but he was already shaking his head.

"It's too dangerous, Taylor," he muttered. "I will not put you in harm's way."

"Fine, I'll put myself in harm's way." I shrugged. "I trust you. I trust you'll be able to save me if this thing attacks. Why don't you trust yourself?"

"So, what? You want to go home? Back to your brother so he can be in the crosshairs too?"

I flinched at the thought. "I can stay with you."

"You cannot stay with me, Taylor," he sighed.

I rolled my eyes. "Right, the lone wolf."

"Right, *wolf*. What part of that do you *not* understand? I am a wolf. I am a danger to you."

"Right now, everything is a danger to me!" I exclaimed.

"All right, all right," Cole interrupted. "Let's all calm down."

I felt my cheeks flush at the reminder of their presence.

"I tend to agree with Taylor. At this point, our best plan is to watch over her on neutral territory," he continued. Harper opened his mouth to argue, but Cole raised a hand to stop him. "I also agree with Harper. Taylor will not be safe staying with him."

This time my mouth opened in protest, but Cole moved to silence me.

"I would offer our abode, but a block of apartments would not be the wisest of choices to lure a predator," he explained.

"And as I believe it's wise for Taylor to stay with one of us four, it leaves one final option."

Hunter's dark eyes widened as realisation struck. "Me? No. No, no, no, no. No."

"No," I agreed. "I think I'll just take my chances."

"It's almost a Full Moon, Hunter," Cole said. "Harper is a loose cannon, just look at him."

Harper was still pacing, his eyes subtly darker somehow, his hands shaking anxiously. He looked wild, animalistic... how could he have changed in the last few minutes?

"Some of us don't have the luxury of controlling who we are, or how we behave," Cole finished.

Harper was shaking his head, but it wasn't in disagreement, it was in release. He took slow, even breaths, and rolled his shoulders, his fists clenching and unclenching. He was trying to calm himself.

Hunter groaned. "Fine, the girl can stay with me."

"How kind," I mumbled.

She hissed and turned towards me, swiping a thick, black paw in my direction that suddenly replaced her quaint hand.

"Do not be ungrateful, human," she warned. "Your days are already numbered."

My breath caught in my throat, and before I could react, Harper was between us, a low rumble in his chest, teeth bared at his comrade. I stumbled back, and found the wall, grazing a thin layer from my forearm.

Ruby sighed. "Cole, do something before she hurts herself again and loses more blood."

Cole tipped his head, and gently brushed his companion's cheek, and she disappeared. Harper looked back at me as I examined my scraped arm, small beads of blood beginning to form on the surface.

"Enough," Cole said. "We have enough to deal with without fighting amongst us like cats and dogs."

Even in my compromised state, I was able to find the humour in his words. This seemed to anger Hunter more, and a low hiss escaped her. Harper pushed his palm against her sternum, and she clutched his wrist.

"What is your fascination with this impotent girl?" she sneered. "Do you not see the trouble she has already caused us?"

"Watch your tongue," he warned. "It is because of that *impotent girl* that I am standing here today."

I frowned.

"So you keep saying." Hunter said harshly. "But is she really worth all this bother?"

Harper looked down his shoulder at me. "It is no bother to me."

Hunter sighed. "Dogs and their loyalty."

"All right," Cole interrupted. "Enough."

"I have said it before, Hunter, if you are not with us, you are of no help to me," Harper sighed. "I will not ask again, but give you the option to leave now."

"I have already said I will not play witness to your suicide mission," Hunter snapped.

Harper shrugged. "So which is it? Stay or go?"

A mixture of anger and loathing flickered across the dark beauty's face, and something else. Betrayal? I bit my lip as I assessed the two shifters, wondering for the first time of the history between them. Jealousy bubbled in my stomach that seemed unreasonable given the circumstances.

"I am with you," Hunter answered quietly. The jealousy rose to my chest.

"Right, now that's settled, I think it's high time we relocate from this less-than-comfortable abode," Cole sighed. "Hunter, can we rely on your hospitality?"

Hunter glanced at Harper and gave one firm nod. "Fine."

*

Hunter lived in a small one-bedroom house east of South Coast City, surrounded by greens and brown of foliage from the nearby state park. It was quaint, like the brunette firecracker, but somehow beautiful in its understated charm.

"Do not touch anything," she said, picking up some clothes from the furniture as she led the way into the lounge room. It was about half the size of mine, and square, with a corner kitchen that ran along the opposite edge of the one we entered.

"Thank you, Hunter," Harper murmured as he placed my bag down beside the solitary couch. "I promise this will not be for long."

Hunter nodded silently, and twisted her hair up, sliding a wooden stick in to hold it there.

169

"You should get some sleep, Taylor," Harper sighed. "You are no doubt exhausted."

I shook my head. "Not really, I don't even know what day it is. I think it was Wednesday night when all this started but—"

"It's Thursday afternoon. You dozed through the morning recovering from the snake incident."

"Right," I replied. That seemed like days ago now.

Hunter exhaled. "So we are here. Now what?"

"I am going to meet up with Cole and Ruby," Harper explained. "We are going to do some night surveillance."

"What about me?" Hunter asked. "What is my job?"

"Your job is to stay here and ensure Taylor does not touch your things," Harper answered with a smirk.

"Babysitting?" she sneered. "For real?"

I shook my head. "I don't need—"

"Taylor, I will not leave you unprotected, and I am not at my full potential until tomorrow evening," Harper said tiredly. "Hunter, please just do this for me. I do not have the energy to argue with you again."

"Fine." She shrugged.

"Um, don't you need rest too, Harper?" I asked.

"I am okay, I will rest when this is over," he replied. "Please don't kill each other."

Hunter raised an eyebrow, and I pressed my lips together. I wasn't sure what I was more afraid of – the flesh-eating cannibal, or the stunning were-panther that stood beside me.

Her smoky eyes turned to meet mine, and she grinned a toothy grin, not dissimilar to a Cheshire cat's, only more unnerving.

Harper disappeared out the front door as her smile faded.

"I suppose you will want me to feed you too?" she mumbled unenthusiastically. The mention of food reminded me of how hungry I felt; I hadn't eaten in almost a day.

"What have you got?" I asked, trying to be polite.

She shrugged. "Some frozen things, chocolate, chips. I am not so sure, I have not really shopped lately. You can help yourself. I am not your carer."

It is an odd thing to hunt through a stranger's food supplies when you know well and good that she'd prefer you starve to death than have to take care of you. Regardless, I managed to find what I needed for nachos and hated myself for every mouthful I ingested. The hunger that I unleashed by eating felt bottomless, and I ended up microwaving some frozen lasagne too. Hunter looked on in amusement as I ate, frowning at the carbohydrates I could almost feel bloating my cells.

"You are an odd human," she mused, biting the corner off an entire block of chocolate.

I glowered at her. "Why?"

"Because you treat food like it is some sacred entity when it's just something that fuels your body."

"Maybe for some, but my messed up body seems to hoard food like it's going to run out."

She shrugged. "Maybe your body is just more efficient than others."

I felt my brows crease.

"Think about it," she offered, putting the block down with half a row chewed. "If you were stranded in the wilderness, and only got food to eat every few days, your 'messed up body' as you put it would save your life."

I considered that concept as she downed a glass of full cream milk.

"That doesn't help me in present society when food is readily available," I answered. "Instead it just makes me fat."

She rolled her eyes. "First world problems."

"Maybe." I shrugged. "But it's all relative."

"Well, consider yourself *relatively* lucky. You can control your problem; you just need to be strong enough to."

I frowned. "So what's your problem then? That you're some incredibly strong and beautiful feline? You can control shifting; you don't need any Moon cycle to change."

She rolled her eyes. "Ignorant human."

"Seriously, *what is your problem?*"

I heard a growling in her chest, not unlike a stalking lioness.

"*You* wouldn't understand," she sneered. "*Please*, food is your biggest problem? Bring me a violin."

"You little bitch," I mumbled.

She hissed. "*I am no dog.*"

And like that, as quickly as a blink, she burst from her skin like a water-balloon popping mid-flight. Her olive skin turned into thick, black fur, and her limbs transformed into a feline figure. Her former clothes fell in shreds to the floor. She roared in a kind of whimper, sounding shameful almost. The stunning animal in front of me shook its beautiful head until all that was left was a human body, clutching her arms across her unclothed chest.

I leant back to retrieve the brown throw rug from the couch and passed it over to her. Hunter barely looked up as she accepted it from me, and pulled it tight around her shoulders.

"I don't need a Moon cycle to change," she said annunciating each word sharply. "But I have no greater control over it than Harper does when the Moon is at its apex."

"Sometimes you just lose it," I murmured. "You're holding on, then you just lose yourself in a moment of weakness, then there's no going back."

Her dark eyes glanced up at me.

"No, you're wrong," she answered. "There is always going back. That's what makes you strong. Once you lose control, it takes strength to rein it back in. Weakness is an excuse that too many people use. We all have control. We just have to exercise it in different ways."

I stared at her for a long moment. She seemed too young for such wisdom, such profundity.

"How old are you?" I asked.

She exhaled. "Cole said I stopped growing when I reached adulthood. He speculates I'm twenty-one in physical years."

"And chronological years?"

Her eyes hardened. "I stopped keeping count... after ninety-four."

"Ninety-four," I repeated, gaping. I let the idea sink in, then swallowed to compose myself. "What happened when you were ninety-four?"

"I met Harper," she replied. "And realised I was not as lonely as I thought."

"So, you've known Harper for a while?"

"Yes, I suppose," she sighed. "Off and on. He likes his own company for a lot of the time."

"Right. But you're… close?"

"As close as he will get to anyone," she answered a little bitterly. "But like I said, he likes his own company."

I wasn't sure whether I was pleased to hear they weren't too familiar or disappointed that she was right about not allowing anyone nearer to him.

"Do not bother falling for him," she said. "Whatever he may feel for you will not last; it never does. He's different to the boys you are used to. Do not get too attached."

I narrowed my eyes. "I am not used to any boys. And I don't see how it's any of *your* business what he does or does not feel for me."

I was aware I was getting territorial, emotional, and loud. I didn't like being told by this beautiful girl that I wasn't enough for Harper. I hated the thought that she could be right, and I realised then that I wanted him to want me. I wanted whatever he felt for me to last. It was then that I had no doubt in my mind that if I'd have met him first – if he was the one to buy me gelato in Italy the day Leo and I met, I would have realised what I knew now back then. He may be imperfect, mysterious,

174

and a lone wolf, but he was someone I felt like I could be myself with. He was someone that I didn't need to think about whether I was the same person now as I was one or two years before because, with him, I was just Taylor; the same Taylor inside as I've always been. Maybe the same Taylor I've always known I was but never seen physically represented until I lost the weight.

When I was with Leo, I was the new Taylor, the confident, and somewhat lost Taylor; and with Brandon, I was the old, insecure, *Jesse's* overweight *sister*. I felt none of that when I was with Harper. No definitions, no stereotypes, nothing but me.

Why had it taken me so long to realise that he was the one all along? Were the other's just safer options? Familiar choices?

"You are right," Hunter sighed, breaking my reverie. "I do not care much what is between the two of you because, as I said, it will not last."

"I happen to think that—"

"Shh," she interrupted.

I frowned. "You don't have to be so ru—"

Her hand flew up to silence me again as her head tipped. Blood drained from my face when I realised Hunter *wasn't* being rude, she was being cautious. She heard something outside. Something out of place.

She hunched over into a ball as if about to rest her head on the table.

"It's here," she whispered.

"What?" I mouthed.

She slunk down from the chair, morphing into her animalistic black fur as two big paws padded on the floor, followed by two more. The blanket fell to the ground around her.

I swallowed, and sat back, feeling nauseated as my beating heart brought the half-digested food up to sit on my chest.

Hunter snarled, her head snapping in different directions as cracking leaves and twigs sounded outside. It was terrifying, the anticipation and the inevitability. I was marked. I was human. I was going to die. It was here for me.

Hunter stalked in front of me, her tail curling around on itself and swishing against my skin – perhaps her way of keeping me in her sight without looking. She needed her eyes for surveillance now.

There was a scratching, a horrible scraping across the windows, then across the back wooden door. My shoulders tightened as panic set in. I couldn't think about the fact that it was only Hunter that stood between me and death by a creature that would tear my flesh from my bones.

The door handle rattled, and Hunter's hackles rose. My hands shook with anticipation as the door squeaked open. I drew a rasped, silent breath, and stumbled back as the creature stared me in the eyes, its orange irises boring into me with an insatiable hunger I seemed to somehow understand. Hunter growled and rumbled, throwing a phantom bite in the creature's direction. It crept across the floor on all fours; its thick, muscled fingers and toes elongated with dense claws. It was a peculiar shade of red, or perhaps burgundy, with a skeletal, yet muscular structure that made it look like its spine was outside its body, peaking up to a head that sat almost level on its shoulder blades. Its face was flat; its golden eyes were beady, and its sharp teeth were bared in an open snare. Its legs and arms were all muscle with thick, visible veins, with only minute traces of its former human form. If it came down to it, it would easily overpower me in a fight. I even began to question how effective Hunter would be against it.

The wendigo crept forward, staring intently on me and only me. To it, Hunter was merely an obstacle for its next meal.

It tipped its head and made a blood-curdling slurping noise, the kind you might hear a toddler make in anticipation of ice-cream, and crawled towards us.

Hunter growled again, lunging forward to snap at its arm, but it was too quick, and it took a swift swipe at her, its crafted claws scratching clean across Hunter's black-furred face. Hunter whined and snarled, turning her head back at me intently before flicking her head towards the creature and the door, and let out a deafening roar. It took me a moment to find my legs, and then I was edging around, leaving as large a margin as I could between myself and the creature. Hunter growled in a kind of impatient manner, before taking another snap at the wendigo, this time, catching its ankle in her teeth.

I took a breath, and then two, then darted for the door, launching off the back step, and pushing off the balls of my feet as hard as I could. Fear gave me adrenaline, which also gave me hope. Maybe Hunter could overcome it. Perhaps I wouldn't die at the fate of the creature that came after me.

And then I heard it.

Padded footsteps that fell too quickly in my pursuit. I pushed harder, my hips and knees protesting with each agonising step. My legs moved too fast for my body, and I knew that one wrong step would ruin me and would mean my demise. I focused on my breathing, the even in and out, dragging it rasped up my dry throat in thirst of oxygen to feed my overworking muscles. I could hear it getting close, the crackle of leaves and debris bringing tears to my eyes, as I cried out in pain and exertion. The moisture burnt in my eyes and blurred my vision. Each breath was painful but necessary. If I stopped now, I would die.

I kept running and, for the first time since embarking on my getaway, realised I didn't know where I was or where I was going. Everything around me was completely foreign and unfamiliar. I had been lost before in Italy and Paris, almost every day I made a wrong turn, and had to find my way back. But this was different, it felt different. Being lost in a familiar place like home made me feel hopeless like I was being betrayed, like my safety blanket had torn in two. I had nothing to do but keep running. Running for my life, and running from my death. Just running to find any kind of aid or protection.

My legs buckled, and I knew that I was running out of time before I would collapse and it would all be over. Finally. The thought of giving up made me want to cry because I would be letting down more than myself. I would be letting down everyone who loved me, and everyone who had been trying to keep me alive. All for nothing. Such is fate.

The steps behind grew closer as my resolve wavered. I drew a deep breath and waited for my time to run out, trying to picture Jesse, or my mum, or my dad's face in my mind before I was taken and killed. I couldn't see them. I couldn't even see April, or Brandon. Brandon who I had lusted over for so long, or even Leo who I dreamed about since meeting him. No, all I saw were those green eyes, his perfect face, and the carved lips belonging to Harper, and the way he looked when I first saw him in the darkness of the trees that first night. I saw the concern in his eyes when I'd told him about my accidents, that in hindsight weren't so accidental, and the eternal sadness on his face when he told me that he was not good for me. I was going to die, and all I could see was him.

It was a fair trade. My life for his. I didn't regret a thing.

A flash of white blew past behind me, and I felt my legs falter as the footsteps behind me stopped. Inertia drove me forward, and I stole a glance over my shoulder, seeing nothing but foliage before I turned back and simultaneously collided with something hard... something that wrapped itself around me... something that was warm and smelled of wood and musk... something that was drawing me towards into its strong hold.

I gasped and then exhaled in desperate relief and utter exhaustion.

"Shh, it is only me," Harper whispered into my hair.

I could hear a strange strangling sound, and after a long moment realised it was coming from me. My legs wobbled like melted jelly and then gave way as I collapsed in Harper's arms.

179

I let my eyes close, and as the darkness coddled me, I wondered if perhaps I had died and this was my afterlife. My body felt as if it was shutting down, or at least going into standby, or a kind of recovery mode. I felt so drained.

"Harper, is she safe?" another voice asked, breaching through my subconscious. It didn't quite fit my dreamy afterlife.

"Yes, I have her," Harper replied. "Did you get it, Cole?"

"It's taken care of," Cole answered. "How is she?"

I heard Harper sigh. "Fatigued."

"Lucky Hunter was able to wound it before went after her," Cole noted, his voice sounding closer as footsteps fell into stride beside us. "Good effort by Taylor to try and outrun it though, that thing wasn't slow."

"I do not want to think about the alternative," Harper murmured.

"She is safe now."

"For now. The wendigo might be gone, but we still need to find the banshee."

"That, my friend, won't be as easy to do," Cole replied after a short pause.

"As easy as what?" Harper sighed. "I will not let her die. Not now, not before she has lived, not for me."

"We can only do the best we can," Cole said. "But for now, you need to rest. Ruby and I can watch her overnight."

"I do not want to leave her," Harper answered, his grip tightening around me. I felt myself smile, even in my half-dazed state.

"We will all stay together," Cole murmured. "Come tomorrow, the banshee may not be our biggest problem."

"You are right, Cole. Maybe I should go."

"Not now. I think Taylor needs you now. We will deal with tomorrow when it comes."

Harper sighed, his chest rising and falling against me. "But it will come."

Cole exhaled. "Tomorrow, Harper."

Phase Eight
The Clutches of Death

Cold hands pressed against my forehead and cheek, stirring me from my reverie. As consciousness sank in, so did the pain and aching of my joints, my legs, my ribs, and my chest.

"Taylor," a soothing, pleasant voice whispered.

It wasn't the voice I wanted to hear, but that was okay. Because I was alive.

My eyes slowly blinked open, readjusting to the light around me. I was back at Hunter's house on the couch. It was Ruby who was kneeling beside me, her hands pressed to my clammy face. They were better than an icepack.

"Where's Harper?" I asked. It wasn't what I was planning to say, but the words formed by themselves. It was what I really wanted to know.

Ruby frowned. "He is with Hunter."

"Oh." I felt myself frown at the news as a new pain seared itself through my chest. It was a selfish thought, considering. "Is she okay?"

"Yes, she will be," Ruby answered thoughtfully. "She got a little knocked around, but she's healing quickly. Cole and

Harper arrived in time to save her from any permanent damage."

I assumed, given Hunter was able to heal quickly, that the kind of permanent damage Ruby was referring to meant death.

"Oh," I sighed again.

It seemed insufficient, but it was all I could think to say. Ruby's silver eyes glistened as she smiled, reaching behind her.

"Here, I think this is yours," she murmured, handing me my phone. "I found it in the back seat of the Jag. It must have fallen from your pocket earlier."

"Thank you," I said, turning it over in my fingers. I unlocked it and saw I had several missed calls and texts from Jesse, Leo, and my parents. I slowly read their concerned words, and hit reply, telling each of them I was fine, I just needed time, and I was staying with a friend.

"Everything okay?" Ruby asked.

I sighed. "Yes. As okay as it can be, I suppose."

"Right." She nodded. "For what it's worth, I understand what it's like to be suddenly deep in the supernatural without warning. The first time I found out vampires existed was when I woke up as one."

"Seriously?"

"Cole saved my life, or rather preserved it. But I had a human life I was more than happy with before this life; one that took a lot to let go of."

I frowned in thought.

"I understand that your situation is a little different to mine, but at least you're still you where it counts," she replied.

"And Harper will see that you can go back to your loved ones, and grow old with them, unlike the rest of us."

I shook my head. "My life wasn't so great before. I didn't feel like me at all anyway. I'm actually almost convinced I don't exist as a person, and that maybe I'm just influenced by the situation I'm in at the time and that alone defines who I am."

"You're still young, you'll find your feet. With time, you'll feel more comfortable in your own skin."

"That's just it. I feel like I'm going to burst out of my skin. I don't know how I'm still together, because I'm thinking so much about things, and it's just too much sometimes, you know? Like, I feel like I need to scream to stop myself from imploding."

Ruby was clearly struggling to relate to my madness, but managed a sympathetic smile. "Things will work themselves out, they always do."

I shrugged. "I wish I could believe you, but I don't. At the moment, I don't know whether I'll be alive next week never mind working through my multitude of issues."

"Yes, you will," Harper's voice interrupted. "As long as I am around."

I looked up, and pressed my lips together in a smile, his mere presence somehow giving me hope.

"Hey," I whispered. "How are you?"

Harper dipped his head. "I am more concerned about your wellbeing."

"I'm very achy."

He smiled weakly. "All things considered, I believe that is the best we can hope for."

"Apparently. How's Hunter?"

"She will be fine. Nothing a bit of time cannot heal."

"Excuse me." Ruby smiled, rising to her feet, and flitting from the room. I tried to pull myself up and managed with a bit of effort. Harper was by my side in two strides.

"You need to rest," he sighed.

I frowned. "So do you. You look terrible."

He breathed a throaty laugh and glanced up at the sun streaming through the window. "The Full Moon is tomorrow. I am affected a day either side."

"All the more reason. Does it hurt?"

He gave a weak cough. "Does what hurt?"

"The Full Moon, changing into a werewolf, you know."

"Yes," he replied. "But it is getting less painful with time."

"How long has it been?"

He glanced at me with recognition. "You have been speaking to Hunter about her experiences."

I nodded.

"I am twenty-eight," he answered.

"So twenty-eight-years-old," I said. "Have you always been this way?"

"Have I always been a werewolf? I have for as long as I can remember, but no. I was not born this way. My father turned me when I was about four, I believe. He was a wolf."

"The tooth?"

"Was his." He nodded.

185

I shook my head incredulously. "Will you always be like this? I mean, look like this? Just because Hunter said she doesn't physically age…"

"That is not the case with my species," he replied. "Which is a perplexing difference between the two."

"I wonder how your genotypes and phenotypes compare," I mused, and then remembered something. "You study molecular biology. Have you ever had a look at them?"

He smiled, seeming impressed. "Yes, I have studied the chromosomes as has Cole who has a medical background, but they do not give much away. I had hoped that, through my studies, I could figure out how… *creations* like Hunter and me are possible. But some things, I suppose, science cannot explain. They are simply supernatural mutations."

"There has to be some kind of explanation," I said.

He chuckled, and then coughed. "Ever the scientist."

"Maybe they are different when you are a wolf to when you are in human form. You'd never be able to check yourself, maybe—"

"No, Taylor," he interrupted sternly. "You cannot be near me when I am a wolf, it is not safe."

"I was before." I shrugged.

"And look how that turned out."

My eyebrows rose. "Not bad for you."

Harper's features darkened. "Sometimes I wish you had not stopped. Then you would not be in danger."

"But you would probably be dead," I answered. "Which is definitely not any sort of a trade-off."

He sighed and brushed his hair off his sweat-beaded forehead. I hadn't noticed before, but it was heating up in Hunter's cabin. In fact, it was sticky – hot and sticky, and humid. The sun had well and truly come up and was heating up the small room. The atmosphere was uncomfortable, like being in a steam room or a sauna. The thickness of the air all around me seemed to strangle my airways, as my lungs tried to capture the oxygen, but never seemed to get enough to satisfy.

"Gosh, it's hot in here." I said.

"That is because the vampires have gone," he replied. "They tend to bring the temperature down a few degrees."

I smiled and ran a finger over the back of his hand. It was like touching a burning ember.

"You're so hot! Why are you so hot?" I asked.

His breaths were shallow and quick. "Full Moon."

I shuffled towards him, ignoring the cramps that protested in my legs. "Can I do anything? Can I get you ice or... or something?"

He closed his eyes and shook his head infinitesimally.

"No," he whispered. "But I probably should not be here."

"No. I don't want you to go."

His eyes opened. "My being here puts you at risk, which negates my duty of trying to protect you."

"I don't care," I sighed, my hand reaching to hover over his burning cheek. "Stay. Please."

"Taylor..."

"Harper." Cole's voice was a murmur but felt as loud as if he had shouted. "Hunter and I are going after the banshee."

Harper looked disturbed by the news.

"Taylor, how are you feeling?" Cole asked.

I sat back. "Warm."

There was a flash and light breeze, and Ruby appeared beside me, coolness instantly radiating from her.

"Sorry," she said.

Hunter appeared behind Cole, looking a little rummaged, but generally okay. Her eyes were not as bright as before, but she managed a twisted smirk.

"Hunter," I sighed. "You're okay."

"Okay," she echoed in agreement. "You too."

I nodded.

"I cannot stay here, Cole," Harper mumbled. "I can feel it. It's strong already."

Cole frowned. "Ruby will stay here. You are free to go if you must."

Harper stood up shakily. "Why don't I go with you and Hunter stay?"

Hunter scoffed. "You are in no condition—"

"*You* are in no condition," Harper growled.

His hands were shaking, and little droplets of sweat gathered over his skin. He did not look well at all, and had visibly and rapidly declined in the last few seconds that had passed. He spluttered a cough and sighed.

A heartbeat of silence fell, and then there was a loud clap as Ruby's foot beat down on the floor by my feet. I jumped and rested a hand on my chest.

"What was that?" I asked.

She smiled sweetly. "Scorpion."

I looked down, and she lifted her foot, the crushed creature's sting reached towards me. Harper made a strangled sound.

"Do what you must, Harper, but the sooner we end the banshee who marked Taylor, the quicker she will be out of direct harm's way," Cole said.

He choked. "I can help."

"You will be more help resting," Ruby answered calmly, placing a comforting yet restraining hand on Harper's wrist. He flinched at the cold but didn't otherwise move. "Let them go."

There was a dull tearing sound as Harper's eyes settled on me, then moved to Ruby, who nodded towards Cole. I glanced over and watched as Cole and a panther-Hunter vanished from the room. I guess that explained the ripping noise.

"Right, now," Ruby sighed. "Who's hungry?"

I bit my lip. "Not you, I hope."

Ruby laughed. "No. I'm sated. Can I make *you* something? Pancakes? Waffles?"

My mouth salivated at the mention of the sugary breakfast options, but reason tackled my resolve. Eggs, I should eat eggs, or porridge, or some sort of grilled protein; but I was famished, and I needed… no, wanted something flavoursome to quench my hunger than the mostly plain portions of protein. I wanted to enjoy food now that, arguably, my days, and possibly minutes, were numbered.

I opened my mouth, but couldn't quite phrase the words. I knew what I should ask for, and I knew what I wanted to ask

189

for. Once upon a time, those two were the same thing. Now, I was fighting a war with myself.

"Two scrambled eggs – one yolk, one white, with low-fat cheese, and a dash of skim milk," Harper muttered. "Or oat bran porridge made with sweetener, and skim milk."

I closed my mouth as the words I should be saying came from Harper. I stared at him in shock and awe as his lips formed a smile.

"I do not know how much of that Hunter has in her kitchen, but there is a convenience store just up the road," he added.

"How convenient," Ruby replied, glancing at me. "Did Harper forget anything, Taylor?"

I shook my head. "No, I, um… no."

Ruby smiled, and flittered into the kitchen, moving in a white blur every couple of seconds as she navigated around the small, but functional, appliances.

I turned to Harper. "How did you…?"

"I watched you for a while, both in France and here," he said in a gruff voice. He paused and let out a weak cough. "You are quite disciplined with your food."

"I need to be." I shrugged. "If I'm not, I tend to overeat. It's sort of all or nothing with me."

He frowned. "What does it matter if you enjoy your food? Are you so concerned about the way you look?"

"I was never happy when I was overweight."

"Are you happy now?"

"Y-yes."

His brows furrowed, and he coughed again; it sounded like a low growl in his chest.

"It's different," I amended. "It's a sacrifice. I may never be able to eat normally again, but I can still eat relatively normally. I just have to be more careful now. In return, I get confidence, and that to me... is more important than the food... stuff."

"I think you are beautiful regardless of what form you take," he said in a hushed, sincere voice.

I leant forward and tipped my head. "Likewise."

He smiled and then flinched with pain as his body contorted awkwardly. He exhaled in a pant and clutched at the chair. My hand reached out to rub his burning shoulder.

"It is not safe for you to be so close to me," he breathed.

"It's not safe for me anywhere right now," I replied. "So I'm fine just where I am."

Ruby had stopped, frozen, and was looking at us in alarm. She seemed to relax as Harper's grip loosened on the furniture.

There was another blur of white, and then she sighed. "Hunter doesn't have a lot. I may need to go and buy a few things."

"Do you want me to go—"

"No," they said in unison.

Harper coughed. "I will go. You stay with Taylor."

Ruby frowned at him. "I don't think you're quite up to it. You stay here. I will only be a few minutes."

"Taylor will be safer with you."

"And South Coast will be safer if you stay here," she answered politely. "I won't be long. You rest."

Harper exhaled. "Take her with you."

"Harper, she is in more danger leaving here than staying with you," she answered. "I don't believe you will hurt her."

"Me neither," I agreed.

He pouted. "I do not wish to take that risk."

"Ruby, you just go," I said. "We're wasting time talking about it when you could have been there and back by now."

Ruby nodded, drawing keys out her pocket, and glanced at Harper. "I will be as quick as I can."

"We will be fine," I replied, as she gave a parting smile, and then vanished.

I inhaled deeply and turned back to Harper who was on the floor with his eyes squeezed closed as he struggled through another burst of agony.

"Harper?" I asked, leaning towards him.

"Stay back," he breathed.

"It's okay—"

"No," he growled through gritted teeth. "Taylor, get the colloidal silver and the dagger from your bag."

I frowned. "What?"

"Do it, now." He panted. "Go."

I looked around, located my bag by the couch, and fumbled at the zip.

"Hurry, please," he whispered, and then moaned in pain.

I rummaged through, taking out the purple bottle, and the silver dagger that I had once pulled from the shoulder of his wolf-form.

"And do what?" I asked.

"Drink… ugh," he cried. "Drink the silver."

I nodded in a kind of panic, and unscrewed the cap, spilling half of it on my lap as I tipped it towards my mouth. It trickled down onto the couch to where Harper gripped the frame. It made a searing sound as it touched his skin. He breathed through it, seeming to use it as an anchor for whatever internal turmoil he was battling.

"I'm sorry," I whispered, wiping his hand. He let out another cry as the silvery dampness sizzled against his heated skin. "Harper."

"The… the dagger." He panted.

"Do you need it?" I asked, holding it towards him.

His head shook in short bursts. "You do. Use it if…" He paused, and exhaled, then yelled as if being tortured.

"If?" I asked, blinking back tears.

"Taylor, you need to get out of here."

"I can't run."

"Lock yourself in Hunter's room," he breathed. "Use the dagger against me if I come at you."

My mouth fell open. "But why would you—?"

"You are marked, Taylor, I can feel the pull," he moaned. "Go."

"Harper, I—"

"Taylor!" he shrieked, losing the internal battle. "GO. NOW."

I froze for a second before stumbling into gear, my legs protesting as I flung them over the edge, and made them move towards the room. I slammed the door, holding the silver dagger awkwardly as my back fell flat against the wood, separating me from a now wailing Harper. The sound of human cries slowly morphed into the howling of a large wolf.

My heart pounded as silence fell, only the dull thud of padded footsteps falling on the wooden floorboards to break it. There was a low growling, then a whimpering, it sounded like there were two wolves – one on the prowl, the other being scolded. Back and forth, back and forth, nails digging into wood. The door rattled, and I gripped the dagger before letting it loosen in my hand. I didn't want to use it, and I made the decision there and then not to.

My shoulder seared with pain, prickling as if it was being torn open again. I stumbled forward as three other things happened simultaneously – the silver dagger fell from my fingers and spun across the floor, the door that was behind me flew open, and the large brown wolf skirted across the floorboards, its nails leaving tracks in the wood in its path.

The Harper-wolf found its feet as I found mine, and as I push myself back against the wall. Harper's eyes were concerned, embodying the sound of the sympathetic wolf that I'd heard. His muzzle, however, was drawn and salivating… hungry.

"Harper," I whispered. "Please."

There was no way else to describe it, but it was as if there was a magnetic pull dragging him towards me, and I understood what he was trying to tell me before about feeling drawn to me because of my being marked. He wasn't in full control of himself, less-so that he was an animal now, a hunter on the prowl. It scared me, but I could see it in his perfectly clear olive-green eyes that it wasn't what he wanted, and that gave me some kind of blind hope.

His paws skidded across the wooden floor as the Harper-wolf advanced on me. My heart beat loudly in my ears as the scratch on my back seemed to pulse with the same intensity. I didn't want to die, but I felt a strange surge of peace wash over me at the passing seconds, and advancing paw-falls. A calming silence ran through me, and I felt resigned in my impending death.

Harper growled involuntarily, and then whimpered, and barked, his eyes flickering towards the spilled dagger on the floor that lay just out of my reach.

"No," I said, shaking my head at him. "I won't hurt you."

He whimpered, and then snarled, stumbling backwards as he forced himself against the fateful hand he had been dealt. He barked again, whipping his head towards the weapon, and I closed my eyes.

"No," I sighed. "If this is my destiny, then so be it. I don't want to hurt you, and I don't regret saving you. I would do it again without a second thought."

Whimper.

Bark.

Scratches.

I could feel his breath, the heat from his muzzle, the wetness from his snarling teeth.

"I wish it was you, Harper," I murmured. "I wish it was you and not Leo that approached me in that café in Italy."

195

Whimper.

Snarl.

Thud, thud, thud.

I opened my eyes and found myself staring into the piercingly hypnotic green eyes of the wolf. Pleading eyes that yearned to be forced closed. But I couldn't do it.

"Make it quick," I whispered. "Please."

This time it was his eyes that closed, but his jaw opened, revealing his razor-sharp teeth. I exhaled slowly and unthinkingly reached out, running my hand down his thick taupe mane. Harper's mouth snapped shut, and he shook his head, losing his footing on the boards as he made for the dagger, and knocked it over towards me. As he did, there was a flash of white, and I half expected to see Ruby coming to my aid, but it wasn't Ruby. It wasn't even Cole.

The hair stood up on my arms as I stared death in the face. The real death. Death that I hadn't seen before, but felt. My shoulder burned with fervent remembrance as the white woman towered over me, ghostly, and skeletal, like a waif. I felt as if the air had been sucked from my lungs as she screamed, her pale almost translucent eyes bore into mine, hypnotising me, drawing me in. My arms went limp, falling to my side, and hitting something cold, something hard, as the fingers of my right hand encircled the grip of the silver dagger.

I tried to lift it, but I felt paralysed, drained, and drowsy as she continued to scream into my subconscious, killing me slowly as my awareness sank into darkness. My eyes rolled closed as her cry cut off, and I heard a rasping growl from

Harper. Struggling against the cloud, I lifted my eyebrows to gain sight and watched as the sharpened ends of the white creature's fingers wrapped around the wolf, puncturing ten holes around its shoulders as she regained her power.

It was enough to rouse me, and I threw my body forward, aiming for her heart, but hoping for any sort of strike that would release my poor Harper-wolf from her clutches of death.

I felt an impact, but couldn't identify where since everything happened so quickly, starting with the dagger going in before my body was pushed back, and I was pinned to the floor by a black panther. My head bounced off the hard boards as I exhaled all the air from my crushed lungs. I could hear ripping and tearing, struggling, and a strange gurgling. I could see nothing but the Hunter-panther snarling over me, and the roof rotating above me. I could feel a throbbing in the back of my head, a cold-wetness down my neck. I couldn't feel my legs or arms.

I closed my eyes and decided that I didn't care. As long as Harper was alive, I didn't care what happened to me; and if he was dead, I cared even less.

*

When I regained consciousness, my head felt squashed, and my hearing was muffled. I momentarily wondered if I was dead, and then decided it wouldn't be this uncomfortable. I could hear though, which was promising. I just couldn't seem to decipher what was being said. I could feel as well. I felt a soft

197

quilt, a gentle squeeze on my arm, and fingers on my pulse. I tried to open my eyes, but they felt too heavy.

I focused harder on hearing and managed to zero in on specific words.

"She will be okay," Cole was saying quietly. "Her vitals sound normal. A concussion is the biggest concern, but she should awaken at any moment. I wouldn't be surprised if she's already alert in there."

I moved my attention from my heavy eyelids to my fingertips and managed to make them twitch. It was almost as liberating as a deep intake of fresh, crisp air.

"Did you see that, Cole?" Ruby's song-like voice asked. "I think she can hear us."

"Taylor?" Cole asked.

I felt myself frown. It wasn't the voice I wanted to hear.

"I just wanted to get her out the way," Hunter said, sounding further away than the other two. "If I knew she would end up out cold for so long—"

"Hunter," Cole sighed. "You did the right thing for the time. Taylor will wake when she's ready."

I waited, straining my ears for any other signs of life. My biggest hope was that none of the three sounded upset. Maybe Harper was healing nearby. Maybe he was beside me. I willed my fingers to move searchingly over the spongy duvet beneath me. I couldn't find anything. My heart sank. My eyes relaxed closed. Nothing was promising about waking up.

"How is he, Hunter? Has he changed back yet?" Ruby asked quietly.

Changed back? Who? Harper? Was he still a wolf? My brain asked questions before I could stop it. So he was alive? That had to mean he was at least alive.

"No, not yet," Hunter murmured. "He is not healing either. I do not know what is wrong."

"Full Moon?" Ruby asked.

Hunter sighed. "It has never been a problem before."

"Perhaps it is the cause of the injuries?" Cole mused. "Maybe direct harm caused by the banshee…?"

Harper was alive, but still hurt, and I was too busy wasting time being unconscious. My eyes opened, and I tried to sit up on Hunter's bed. Two sets of cold hands pushed me back down.

"Where is he?" I asked, pushing them away.

"You need to rest," Cole answered.

I frowned. "I've had plenty. Where is Harper?"

"Taylor, there is nothing you can do," Ruby said. "You're best to rest."

I laid back. "I might be able to help, I've helped him before. I'm studying to be a vet."

There was a low howl from the next room, and I sat up again, this time ignoring the hands that urged me to stay put.

"Hear that? He needs me," I sighed. "Let me go. Please, I promise I'll sleep when I know he's okay. Please, Cole."

He stepped back in defeat, and I shuffled to the end of the bed, feeling my head spin and pulse to a nauseating degree, but ignored it. All I could hear was Harper's soft, but agonised breathing; it was the most profound sound in my world.

199

I looked around, but couldn't see him anywhere. My heart reacted in a yearning, panicking, and my lungs struggled to inflate. It was just like when Hunter's panther-paws were clamped down on them.

"He's on the couch, Taylor," Ruby replied.

I drew in a ragged breath and stumbled towards the door. My legs felt worn, and my back was sore, my head throbbed with rising pressure, and my chest struggled to expand. But nothing was going to stop me from finding Harper.

"Harper," I whispered, closing the canyon-like gap that stood between me and the couch. My hands grasped it before I fell, and I pulled myself over the rest of the way. That was when I saw him, lying helpless with dried blood crusted onto his coat. I wondered why no one had bothered to clean him, and then nearly cried when I deduced it was because they were too busy taking care of me. I was their mission, their priority. Harper had seen to it that it remained that way, even if it meant he suffered for it.

I blinked back tears I hadn't realised were there, and crawled around to the front of the couch to better get to him. His eyelids opened and closed slowly, but seemed to widen when he saw me. Those eyes – those perfectly clear green eyes.

"Hey," I sighed and felt a salty-droplet fall from the end of my nose.

I ran my fingers through his fur, and he closed his eyes, letting out a quiet moan. I could see the puncture marks from the banshee's fingers, which seemed to ooze with each slow thrum of his heart.

"Why aren't you healing?" I asked. "There's no silver in it."

"What about the Weavers?" Ruby said. "Rob, Harper's godfather is one, isn't he?"

I looked up. "What is a Weaver?"

"Shadow Weavers are… I guess you could liken them to witches," Cole explained. "I don't know what they can do, but we can call them."

"Did you get it?" I asked, sitting back on my heels. I was getting used to the muscle ache now. "The banshee, I mean?"

"Yes." Cole nodded. "You struck quite true with the silver dagger."

"So I'm not marked any more?" I sighed, reaching to feel my shoulder. My skin felt completely smooth as if I'd never been scratched at all. I had thoroughly healed.

"He's supernatural," I whispered. "He's not healing because he's supernatural."

Ruby, Cole, and Hunter blinked blankly at me, but it was Hunter who spoke.

"What are you on about?" she huffed. "And what does Harper being supernatural have to do with anything?"

"Cole, what happens when you bite a human?" I asked, ignoring Hunter's questioning.

Cole frowned. "Taylor, I don't—"

"Please, it's important," I replied.

"Well, vampires are venomous, so we either drain the human to death or turn them," he answered slowly. "They can walk away if we're careful not to excrete the venom, but unless the vampire has control, it's unusual. Why?"

I nodded. "What happens if you were to bite a werewolf then?"

Knowledge seemed to glow in his silver eyes.

"In the unlikely occurrence that was to happen, turning them would be impossible," he replied. "And so would draining them, since their blood is different from a pure human or canine. Death would be the most likely outcome."

"And if a banshee was to… m-mark a supernatural being?" I said. "Maybe death isn't just inevitable… m-maybe it's instantaneous."

Cole and Ruby seemed to get paler than their regular ashen appearance.

"I'll call Rob and Ebony," Cole murmured, his lips hardly moving. "If Taylor's theory is correct, they might be our only hope."

I felt the blood drain from my face at the validation of my speculation and leant in closer to the Harper-wolf who was taking short, shallow breaths as his eyes rolled open and closed.

"You're going to be fine," I whispered. "If I have to live, so do you."

Cole began to pace.

"This sucks," Hunter exploded. "What was the thing doing going after him to begin with anyway?"

"There's a point," Ruby mused. "What was hunting him?"

I continued to stroke his fur, far from his wounds.

"Something with a silver dagger with a *wolf's-eye* stone embedded in it," I replied.

Cole stopped pacing. "Wolf's-eye?"

"That's what it's known as, or a Moonstone." I shrugged. "I looked it up."

Cole's brow puckered, and he walked over to look Harper in the eye.

"Harper, that night you were being hunted by someone. Did you recognise them?" he asked. "Blink once for yes, twice for no."

Ruby and Hunter stepped closer to see Harper's answer.

Harper closed his eyes and then opened them again, and we waited in anticipation to see if he was confirming that there was someone out there that knew about werewolves, and that was hunting them, here, in South Coast.

His eyes glanced up at me.

"What? No," I sighed. "How could it be me?"

"I don't think he means you," Cole murmured. "I think he means you know who it is."

"How would I know?" I frowned. "Since I've been back, the only people I've really seen are my brother Jesse, April, Brandon, and then Leo when he arrived."

Harper moaned.

Cole's brow creased. "Who's Leo?"

"A guy I met in Italy." I replied. "You don't think—"

"When did he arrive in South Coast?"

"A few days ago, maybe a week. I can't remember."

Harper whimpered as he moved his head.

203

I glanced at him, and then back at Cole. "There is no way it could have been Leo. Harper had been in the same café as him in Italy, and nothing happened. Plus, Leo was still in Italy when I left."

Harper made a noise that sounded like disagreement.

Cole tipped his head. "What makes you so sure?"

I sighed. "Because he saw me off at the airport! There is no possible way he could have—"

I stopped as the thought struck me at the same moment as what could only be described as motion sickness washed over me.

"What is it?" Ruby asked, wide-eyed. I looked up at the three of them who were looking back at me with varying expressions. Cole was curious, Ruby was concerned, Hunter was furious.

"I... I was delayed at a stopover on the way back for almost a day," I whispered. "I suppose, if he was on another flight it's possible..."

"Well, Harper managed to beat you back here, of course it's possible, you silly girl," Hunter sneered..

I felt the blood drain from my face. It was true that the wolf had been there on the side of the road when Jesse was driving me home. Harper could have left after me if he was watching me, and caught the next flight.

I looked back at the wolf and brushed his ear as he peered up at me. I could see it in his eyes.

Harper was watching me.

Leo was watching Harper.

I left Europe.

Harper left Europe.

Leo left Europe.

I was delayed.

They weren't.

Harper waited for me to land.

Leo found Harper and struck.

The banshee showed up as the countdown to Harper's death started.

I showed up and took his place.

"Oh, no," I sighed. "It was Leo, wasn't it?"

It made sense now – the way Harper seemed to disappear at Leo's presence, the subtle warnings he had dropped: *'while he may be capable in protecting you from… from some things, he's not the one for it on this occasion'*.

I let out a low sob. "Oh, I'm such an idiot."

"Well, we know *that*," Hunter mumbled. It somehow sounded harsher in her Spanish accent.

"Hunter," Ruby warned, at the same time Cole asked. "What is it, Taylor?"

I wasn't sure what was more hurt, my body, my heart, or my ego. Leo hadn't flown here to take me out at all. He had flown here to hunt and kill Harper.

I shook my head. "I just feel responsible. I should have seen it, I think Harper was trying to warn me about Leo."

"How could you have known?" Ruby asked. "Harper didn't tell anyone there was a wolf-hunter in town."

"I know, but—" I started then lost my words as suddenly there was a puff of fire-coloured smoke, and two figures appeared amongst it. I jumped, and then exhaled.

"Rob, Ebony," Cole sighed. "Thanks for coming."

I wasn't sure what I was expecting when Harper mentioned his godfather, but maybe someone older-looking than his mid-twenties. Rob was tall, with a brown tousled hair, and brilliant deep blue eyes. Beside him stood a petite, but flawless, raven-haired beauty, with piercing blue eyes, and full lips, not looking much older than I was. My ego took another beating.

"We shouldn't have called, but we don't know what else to do," Cole explained quickly. "It's Harper. He's not healing."

Rob frowned at the wolf beneath my fingertips. "What's happened? Silver bullets?"

"No, a banshee got a hold of him," Cole replied. "I've tried stitches, and human remedies, but his body rejects them. We weren't sure if there was anything you could do that we can't."

"A banshee?" Ebony murmured. "How? Why?"

"This one brought a huntsman to South Coast," Hunter said, jutting her chin in my direction. "He was protecting her when the banshee struck."

My head was shaking, but it was Cole who came to my defence.

"Actually, Taylor managed to wound the banshee with a silver dagger," he replied. "It sounds like the hunter, Leo, was tracking him all the way from Europe."

206

Rob walked around to kneel beside me. "I… I don't know whether there is anything we can do. I've never tried to heal anyone before, especially someone supernatural. My foster-son, Joel, did once, but he's part Light Lacer, and she was a pure Lacer. They're a different breed of supernatural."

"What about a spell or something?" Ruby asked.

Rob looked hopeless as he shrugged. "We can only try."

"That's all we're asking," I whispered.

Rob looked at me properly for the first time. "You're Taylor. Harper has mentioned you."

I looked back at him through tear-filled eyes. "He's mentioned you too."

Rob nodded. "Do you mind giving us some space, Taylor? You can stay close, but—"

"Sure," I sighed, shuffling around to the side, so I was by Harper's head. His slow-blinking eyes followed my movement, and he gave a quiet moan as his neck looked up.

"Ebony, come in close," Rob murmured, taking one of her hands, and moving the other one over Harper's wounds, he parted the fur to see the damage and winced. "I really hope this works."

"We'll give it our best shot," Ebony said, clutching her husband's hand tighter. They glanced at each other, and each gave a defiant nod, holding their free hands over him as their eyes closed in concentration. Not a breath was heard as the four of us watched on in silent desperation.

Heartbeats passed, and there is no sign of anything. I've never been a particularly patient person, but this was just painful. My teeth sank deeper into my lower lip.

"Rob, I can't..." Ebony said breathlessly.

Rob shook his head, his eyes remaining shut. Ebony exhaled in a gasp as blood trickled from her nose. She released Rob's hand and panted hopelessly.

"I can't even feel it penetrating, it's like there's a bubble around him," she sighed.

"That's it?" I frowned. "That's all you can do?"

"I'm sorry, Taylor," Rob murmured. "Believe me, if there was anything else—"

"What about another spell or... or something?" I said. "You can't just let him *die*."

Rob shook his head. "He heals differently to us. He has his own healing properties in his blood to what we do in ours, there's—"

I lunged forward. "What if they mixed?"

"What?" Rob asked, and I heard the same echo from Cole behind me.

I shook my head. "The blood, your blood, and Harper's blood," I explained, sounding like a crazy person grasping at straws. "The vampires heal by their venom, so if they were to bite him, he'd die. But you just said you and he... werewolves and Weavers, both heal through the blood. Harper is still part human, what if giving him a transfusion of your blood acted as a kind of antigen?"

208

Rob and Ebony exchanged looks of bewilderment, so I turned my attention to Cole, as a doctor, to see if I was making any sense.

Cole's brow was set in thought. "It may work."

"We've got to try," I sighed, glancing at Harper as his eyes drooped closed. I couldn't bear the thought that his blinks were numbered. "Please, we're running out of time."

I turned back to Rob and Ebony. "Say you'll do it. We shouldn't need much, not... not if we inject it around his wounds. Right, Cole?"

Cole shrugged. "It does sound like a reasonable theory, given the similar healing qualities between the two genera."

"All right." Rob nodded, rolling up his sleeve. "Let's do this."

Cole disappeared in a flash, and then was back by Rob's side with a syringe. Rob was removing his belt to use as a tourniquet, then began pumping his fist. Ruby covered her nose discretely while Hunter leant forward. I rested my hands on either side of Harper's slumped face.

Cole moved with practised precision, easily finding Rob's vein, and carefully filled up the cylinder.

"I've got another one, but I don't want to take too much of your blood just in case it's unsuccessful," Cole explained as he flittered around to get a better angle of Harper's wounded neck. "Everyone cross their fingers that this works."

The next seconds that passed felt longer than any other I had ever experienced in human existence. The syringe of thick blackish-red liquid was emptied into the dying wolf, and Cole frowned in concentration as we waited and watched.

"He can't die," I cried. "Cole, he can't die."

Cole's intense silver eyes glanced up at me. "It was a solid theory, Taylor, but—"

"Look!" Hunter gasped. "They are closing. He's healing."

I inhaled sharply and leant closer as the puncture wounds shrank before my eyes. I felt giddy and lightheaded with relief, so much so that I thought I might pass out. I didn't though, and for that I was grateful. Instead, I sat by Harper, stroking the length of his muzzle from his eyes to his nose as he slowly relaxed into sleep. I rested my head on the arm of the couch, and listened as the rasping, pained burst of breath became slower, even inhales. I didn't care that my body ached to the point of numbness, or that the guy I had fallen for, and who I thought travelled across the world to see me, was in fact only here to hunt werewolves. The only thing I cared about was that Harper was healing and that he would be okay. As far as I was concerned, the rest of the world could wait.

*

"Taylor," the most beautifully accented voice whispered, as warm fingers stroked the length of my cheekbone.

I awoke with a start and winced as my tightened muscles protested, and my still-wrapped head squeezed with pressure.

"Harper!" I sighed. "You… you… you're."

His lips pulled up in a twisted smile. "Hi."

210

I smiled back as my breath caught in my swollen throat, and became hysterical-sounding sobs of relief. "Hi."

"Hi," he replied.

I threw myself forward onto him without thinking, and he flinched under me.

"Easy." He chuckled but hugged me back. "I am still on the mend."

I laughed lightly, and sat back, realising for the first time that he was mostly naked. He only had a blanket around his waist to conceal him. I felt my cheeks blush as my heart stuttered. Harper saw me looking and glanced at me in amusement.

"Wolves do not require clothes," he noted.

I swallowed and shook my head to clear it, forgetting it hurt to do so. "Right."

"How are you feeling?"

"How am *I* feeling? How are *you* feeling?"

"I asked you first." He smirked.

"I'm better now." I shrugged. "Now I know you're okay. Harper, I—"

"Taylor," he sighed. He paused, looking conflicted, then looked down. "When the Full Moon passes, I need to leave South Coast."

I sat back. "What?"

"It's not safe for me here, and it's not safe for you if I'm here," he answered. "The last few days… that was too close a call. You almost died, I almost died, Hunter was put in danger, and Cole, Ruby… Rob…"

211

"No, Harper, you can't leave," I said. I felt like I had fallen from cloud nine, and plummeted straight to rock bottom. "I can't, you can't... I, I need you here... with me."

Harper looked down, his fingers reaching to brush my hand. "From the beginning, I made it clear that you and I... I'm just not sure if things will work out for the better in the end. You should be with someone else, someone normal."

"Someone like Leo?" I asked. "Or do you mean someone like Brandon? Because he's the only *normal* guy in my life at the moment who I'm not related to."

Harper shook his head.

"Why didn't you tell me about Leo? That he was the one, the hunter that stabbed you that night?"

"I wanted you to make up your own mind about him," he replied. "Besides, the fact he is equipped to fight the supernatural is probably a good thing."

"Good? He is the reason we were all in danger! If he hadn't attacked you, the banshee wouldn't have shown up, and I wouldn't have been marked, and *none* of this would have happened!"

"Taylor, calm down," Harper murmured, reaching up to run his hand down my cheek. The tears pooled in my eyes, and I shook my head.

"It just doesn't seem fair," I whispered. "Don't you want to stay with me?"

Harper's head rocked from side to side, and I let out a sob. Rejection hurt more than any muscle ache.

"It's... it's not that simple," he answered. "Taylor..."

I sniffled. "No, I get it."

"I'm sorry."

"So… will you go back to London, or France?"

"I have not decided yet, but probably neither," he replied. "I think a fresh start is called for."

"Of course," I mumbled, wiping the wetness from my cheeks. As I did, I felt the bandage that was still around my head and began tugging at it.

"No, leave it on," Harper said.

"Please don't touch me," I sighed. "I want it off."

Hurt flickered in his eyes, but he sat back conforming to my request. I finished removing the gauze and felt the bump and tape at the back of my head. It was clearly the culprit for the dizziness and cold oozing from earlier.

"So what now?" I asked, rolling the gauze around my hand.

Harper was silent for a moment, so I looked up. He seemed indifferent like he was trying hard to not show any ounce of emotion.

"If you would like to gather your things, I can get Hunter, or the vampires, to drop you home," he replied. "You should be safe now that the wendigo and banshee are gone. Well, as safe as you ever were before being marked."

He gave a light laugh that made me frown.

"You will be okay, Taylor," he said. "Smile."

I shook my head. "I can't."

He sighed, and slowly reached up to press a thumb on my chin. My lips parted as Harper stared into my eyes. It was the most intimate moment I'd ever shared with anyone; like a conversation spoken with nothing but a look, a twinkle in his eye, the unsaid words that shouted volumes. Harper's lips parted in response, and my eyes followed the movement, before returning to see his focus fall to my lips, and then return to meet my eyes again. Seconds passed as the electricity charged around us, then, quicker than I was ready for, his hand dropped back to his lap together with his gaze.

"Cole, Ruby?" he murmured.

At the mention of their name, the two appeared at the side of the couch as if they'd been there all along.

"Harper?" Cole answered.

Harper's head rose, as his sight caught mine again. "Would you please take Taylor home?"

I opened my mouth to protest as Harper's eyebrows lifted, then thought better of it, so closed it again.

"Be safe," Harper sighed.

I tried to nod. "You too."

I stood up, and carefully gathered my bag.

"You will be okay, Taylor," he said.

I swallowed the lump that had developed in my throat. "We'll see."

"I truly am sorry."

I shrugged. "Such is fate."

Epilogue
Super Natural

The weeks that followed were some of the toughest and longest I had ever experienced, which included the time it took me to lose weight. I tried to forget what had passed, but I couldn't. I decided to focus on uni and getting my health back on track, but even that felt trivial after staring death square in the face. I also tried getting back into a kind of normal by having coffee dates with any guy that asked me, but none of them made it past a first meeting. Staring into the eyes of strangers, I felt nothing, and that made me feel lonelier than I'd ever experienced before. As days stretched on, the void in my life and in my heart grew, and I began to care less and less about everything that I once valued. I gained back two of my lost kilos, and couldn't locate the drive or passion to drop them. Instead, I tried to do what I could to make it through the long, impossible days.

Jesse began to worry. He even tried talking April and Ashley into taking me out, but it really just encouraged them to bond over their shared dislike of me. So I left to brood on my own at *Clair De Lune*, the café Harper had once taken me.

Brandon moved on too, to another couple of girls who occupied him for a while, but in the end weren't enough to keep his eyes from wandering. Everything was normal to a painful degree, but maybe 'ordinary' was a better word for it. It was like waking up in black and white after living in a dream of technicolour. My life and time with Harper may not have been smooth sailing, but I had never felt more alive or more compelled by life than when I was with him.

Leo disappeared too. He left, but I was glad. He was there at my house the morning that Cole and Ruby had dropped me home.

"Taylor, I am glad that you are okay, I was so worried," he said, throwing his arms around me after Jesse had finally finished giving me a once over. He was concerned about my head but passed the first aid I had been administered.

"Leo, why are you here?" I murmured, stiffening in his embrace.

He pulled back to study my face. *"I was worried. You just disappeared after our talk."*

"Yeah, about that…" I sighed. *"I'm not yours, Leo. I'll never be yours. I belong to someone else, someone that acts to protect, instead of harm."*

"I do not understand what you mean." He blinked. *"Taylor, you are not speaking sense."*

"When did you arrive in South Coast, Leo?" I asked.

Leo's dark brow drew curiously. *"I am not sure I know what you mean."*

"*Just what I said,*" I replied. "*I want to know when your plane landed in South Coast.*"

"*I do not know what this has to do with anything.*"

I exhaled slowly. "*Okay, then answer me this: why did you really come to South Coast?*"

He smiled, but it didn't reach his eyes. "*I told you this – to take you out properly.*"

"*Stop lying,*" I whispered. "*I know what you did, I know why you're really here… I know what you are.*"

Leo's eyebrows dropped, causing his eyes to darken. "*What do you know?*"

"*Everything,*" I answered. "*So, you might as well know that there's no point in staying in town. You have no business in South Coast any more.*"

His eyes narrowed. "*Is that right?*"

I nodded rigidly, and Leo smiled. "*So the dog is dead? My condolences, I know you were attached, or rather he was attached to you.*"

I clenched my jaw, and tried to hide the disgust I felt as I looked at him. He was the first man I let my guard down around, the man I had trusted so quickly and entirely. For the first time since saying goodbye to Harper, I was glad that he'd left me feeling so dishevelled and beaten because it meant my story was easier to believe. It meant that Leo would really and truly leave Harper alone; it gave him his freedom.

"*You make me sick.*" I said. "*How can you be so full of hate?*"

"*Do you not think you are taking your love of animals a bit far now, Taylor?*" he asked cockily. "*I thought even you had standards.*"

"*He was twice the man you are.*"

217

Leo shook his head. *"He was half the man I am... quite literally."*

"Get out," I whispered. *"And don't come back."*

He smirked and turned to leave. *"Apparently, there is no need."*

That was the last I saw of Leo, which at least was a small ray of light in my perpetual darkness. Though, the memory of him still makes me feel sick to my stomach. To think that anyone could be so cold and destructive, just for the sake of being, was so dumbfounding to me, especially towards someone as kind and gentle as Harper. Maybe I was biased, maybe I only remembered him as the guy who was always there to save me from one of the many things trying to kill me, but that didn't negate the fact that *he was there*. If there was one thing that got me through, that kept my lungs inflating, and my heart beating, it was the memory that he once cared about me enough to risk his life for mine over, and over. Even in times of doubt, when my mind tried to remind me that he was merely repaying the debt he felt he owed me for saving his life, I couldn't ignore the fact that he stuck around and watched over me like a guardian, an angel, my saviour.

I owed him so much, yet without him, I wasn't sure whether the gift of life he'd given me was a fair trade. I missed him so much it was painful, and I could barely comprehend the weight of the emotion I felt for him, because it seemed to sneak up on me, and then encapsulate me, paralyse me. It hurt, but I welcomed the pain because it was a reminder that he was real, that it was all real, and that he was out there somewhere.

As days continued to pass, and wounds healed, it began to get harder. I started to forget little things about him – the crease of his smile, the shine of his taupe hair, the rhythm of his walk… the little details slowly began to slip away. Then it got worse, and the memories faded further. The way he looked at me, the sound of his accent… the flecks of olive-green in his eye. As these memories faded, I seemed to fade too. I began to exist like a zombie: sleep, eat, work, study, eat. *Eat.* My health began to worsen, and my self-confidence dropped as self-consciousness grew. In five weeks, I was now nearly six kilos heavier than I was upon my return to South Coast, and although I wasn't nearly as bad as I once was, I could see rock-bottom in sight.

I tried, for Jesse's sake, and for my Mum and Dad, to get back on track, and pull myself out of the slump, but my heart wasn't in it, and although I managed to lose a kilo or two, I was still a long way to being the way I was.

So I persevered, getting by where I could, and trying in vain to picture Harper whenever I had the chance to close my eyes. It wasn't an ideal way to live, but it got me through each day by painful day.

And then one day, two weeks later, my mundane routine changed.

I didn't even see it coming.

The day started like any other – up, shower, eggs, porridge, diet coke, out the door. Uni, classes, library…

Then I perched myself on the side of the road waiting for Jesse to come and pick me up. I waited… and waited. Half an hour passed, which turned into an hour, then another forty-five minutes. I called him four times, then gave up and decided to just walk. I assumed that he had probably been called into a last minute surgery now that he was in the emergency medicine rotation.

I dragged my feet as I walked, cursing internally that today was the day I'd decided to hire out all my secondary reading books from the library. My bag felt heavier with every step, and I wondered whether I would do permanent damage to my posture. At least it got my heart pumping, it was the most alive I'd felt in weeks.

I was just over halfway home when the strap broke off, scattering the books, and contents of my bag, up the curb and on the road like a final hard kick in the side. I began to gather my belongings, not caring about incoming traffic as I stretched onto the bitumen for my lip-gloss and wallet. It was these types of things that startled me most – my complete lack of care for my own wellbeing. It was something that had been fought for by four supernatural beings just seven weeks prior.

I bundled everything back into the broken bag, and tucked it under my arm, continuing on my journey home after what now felt like the longest day ever.

"Excuse me, miss?"

The voice had come out of nowhere and jarred my joints. My lungs ceased to function, as my brain processed whether I had actually heard the French-English accented words, or whether I was now hallucinating while awake. Seconds passed as I deliberated on whether to turn until finally deciding it was worth the shot to see whether I *was* crazy or not.

Harper tipped his head as I stepped around.

"You dropped this," he said.

It took me a moment to believe what I was seeing. Harper. It was really Harper. Standing there all tousled hair, and olive-green eyes, holding my student identification card between his index and middle finger.

"It's you," I murmured. "It's really you?"

"Taylor Mistry, always losing your identity," he sighed. "Whatever are we going to do with you?"

I opened my mouth, but it took me a moment to form any coherent words.

"You're... you're back?" I asked.

"I never left."

"You... What? Why? Why didn't you... I've been..."

"I know." He frowned, looking at the floor. "I have been watching you. You have not kept your side of the bargain. I told you to be safe... you said you would be okay."

"*You* said I'd be okay. I said 'we'll see'."

"Right."

I looked down and found myself crying. "I can't believe you're here. I've dreamt of the moment I'd see you again. I planned what I would say, and what I would do, and now I'm just blank and numb."

Harper watched me silently while I processed everything.

I shook my head incredulously. "Leo left, he... he thought you were dead, and I let him think you were. I thought it would

221

give you the best shot of getting away," I said. "And I haven't seen Cole, or Ruby, or Hunter again since… after that forty-eight hour period of crazy, everything and everyone just seemed to disappear, and I was all alone."

Harper frowned. "Thank you for how you handled Leo. I had Hunter tail him to ensure he left, which is why I decided to stay. As for leaving you alone, that was my call. I wanted to give you the chance of a normal life, and it both pleased and pained me to see you at least try and move on."

"Pained? Why?" I asked.

Harper shook his head. "It is not fair to say, but seeing you with those other guys… let's just say it was challenging to stay hidden at times."

I felt my heart breaking. "I never wanted to see anyone else. I wanted you, Harper, but you left. You left me. You didn't want me any more. So no, it's not fair for you to say that to me."

"I truly am sorry, Taylor," he murmured. "Maybe this was a bad idea."

He took a step as if to leave, and panic surged from my centre to my temples.

"Why did you come back?" I asked. "Why now?"

He thought for a moment. "It was hard for me too, you know."

"No," I whispered. "I didn't know."

He looked up. "All I ever wanted for you was your happiness, and I failed at that in every turn. In Italy, and when I came here. My mere presence in your life has brought nothing

222

but danger and chaos. How could you want that? How can you want me, when all I do is complicate your life?"

"You never complicated my life," I replied. "You completed it. You gave a reason for being; you helped me live, really live my life as if it was really something to be cherished. Looking back over the last few months, I never regret stopping that car and helping you that night. What I do regret is letting you send me away that day without telling you, that without you, my life isn't worth anything."

Harper was shaking his head sadly. "How can you say that? You are so gifted, you are surrounded by good people, you live in a safe place, and have a good education, you are young and beautiful, and—"

"None of that means anything," I sighed. "I don't feel it. I don't feel anything except pain and darkness without *you*, Harper. When you left, you took my heart with you, and I have *tried... I have tried* so *hard* to move on, but I don't want any of it, because all I want is you."

He swallowed as pain flickered across his face. "Taylor..."

I let out a sob, and crouched down, dropping my heavy bag at my feet as I crumpled into a ball; it was easier to breathe when my lungs didn't need to inflate so much.

"I can't keep doing this," I cried. "I can't. I don't want to. I can't."

"Please don't cry," he whispered. His voice was closer now, and between the gaps in my fingers, I could see his black shoes in front of me.

"Please don't go."

I felt his hands on my shoulders as he lifted me up standing. My head rolled back as the fresh air stung the wetness on my cheeks. I must've looked like a wreck.

Harper's fingers brushed my face, carefully wiping away some of the tears that stained them. His lower lip pulled in contemplatively as he assessed my features, and then he sighed again.

"Whatever are we going to do with you?" he asked again.

I shrugged awkwardly beneath his warm fingers. "You could bite me."

His brow twitched in a pucker. "Please tell me that you are not serious."

"If that's all that's holding you back, that you're afraid you'll hurt me, then turn me into a wolf," I whispered. "We could be the same, and you'd never have to worry about me again. Problem solved."

His grip loosened as he shook his head sadly. "That is not a solution."

"So, you're saying we can never be together then?" I asked. "That you just came back so you could leave again, and I have to go through all the pain of m-missing you again?"

"Taylor, why can't you see that there is no need for you to change for anyone?" he murmured, brushing the back of his fingers down my cheek. "You are enough."

"Not for you."

"*I* did not say that," he replied, and there was that look in his olive-green eyes again. That adoring, the-rest-of-the-world-

224

doesn't-exist look that made it feel like a lightning storm was developing between us.

I blinked. "I… don't… understand."

"I like you the way you are, Taylor," he answered. "Not for the way you look, but for who you are. You are enough."

I felt the confusion on my face as I tried to work through what Harper was saying, and exactly what that meant. He liked me the way I was, but not because I was slim or pretty, but because I was me. *He* thought I was enough. He didn't want me to be anyone or anything else.

"Please tell me what you are thinking," he sighed. "The silence is very unnerving."

I looked up at him. "You like me."

"Yes." He nodded.

"Just as I am."

"Yes."

"Does that mean you're not leaving again?" I asked.

"I told you. I never left before," he replied.

"But you're staying," I clarified, and then added hopefully, "…with me?"

His light green eyes twinkled in the sunlight as he smiled down at me. "I am staying."

I smiled. "Okay."

"Okay." He chuckled, tucking my hair behind my ear.

"But what about the Moon?" I asked.

"What about the Moon?"

"Are you just going to repeat everything I say?"

He laughed. "No."

I bit my lip. "I just… I guess I'm just wondering what has changed since you said things wouldn't work out, and I should… I should be with someone… else."

"You should," he replied. "But that does not seem to work for either of us, does it?"

"So, even though every month you're going to turn into a wolf, you want to stay with me because you like me, just the way I am."

"Because I love you the way you are," he amended. "And if that means for three days every month I need to lock myself up to keep you safe, I will because I will still have twenty-five of them to show you *how much* I love you."

I smiled in complete and utter elation. "And how much is that?"

"Taylor," he sighed. "*Je t'aime, je t'adore, à la lune et retour.*"

"To the Moon and back," I murmured, translating his perfect French. "I love you and adore you too."

Harper grinned, his hand extending over my cheek before running down my neck, to my shoulder, down to rest on my waist.

"How did you know I would be back?" he asked. "What made you so sure?"

I exhaled and felt as though a weight had been lifted and my lungs could finally inflate again.

"Call it wishful thinking," I said.

He nodded. "Wishful thinking."

His lips pulled into a heart-stopping smile, and his arms wound around me, binding my body against his, as he gently lifted me up towards his lips.

"Such is fate," he whispered huskily, before his lips enclosed over mine in our first, electrically charged, and long overdue kiss.

The world could have exploded, could have stopped, or frozen over, we wouldn't have noticed. All I could think of was how much I loved him, how much I needed him, and how our lips seemed to move in perfect unison, binding us together as if completing the whole.

At that moment, we weren't a human and a werewolf. We weren't the two people who found it uncomfortable in our own skin, and in our separate worlds – the natural, and the supernatural. At that moment, we were just Taylor and Harper, in a world of our own, where we would conceivably stay for many moons.